Published in 2012 by Marplesi

Copyright © Sinclair Macleod 2012

ISBN 978-0-9566983-7-7

A catalogue record for this book is
available from the British Library.

The Killer Performer

A Reluctant Detective Mystery

by

Sinclair Macleod

Marplesi Books

Also available by Sinclair Macleod

The Reluctant Detective

The Good Girl

Dedication

In memory of Alison Graham, teacher, friend,
inspiration and the lady who introduced me to
Raymond, Dashiell and Ross.

As always, in memory of Calum, my wonderful
son and constant guiding light.

Acknowledgements

Without these people I would not be able to do what I do.

A big thank you once again to Kevin Cuthbert and George Mitchell for their continued advice regarding police procedures.

Thanks again to the wonderful people at the mortuary in Dundee. In particular Alison Beaton and Dr Priyanjith Perera who were kind enough to offer their advice and knowledge.

As always the mistakes that occur in these pages regarding any of these subjects will be entirely mine.

I keep thanking him and hope I will always be in the position to say cheers to Andy Melvin, who continues to edit these books with great skill and patience. I also offer a big thank you to Karen, who allowed him to use some of his spare time to work on this manuscript.

As always my love and thanks also go to my wonderful wife, Kim and my beautiful daughter, Kirsten. I could not write these books without their continued love and support.

CHAPTER ONE

The cell door slammed with the ominous clang of a mourning bell, the police officer turned the key and the locking mechanism ground out a final turn; I was imprisoned. I was left alone to consider how within two days I had gone from a normal, law abiding citizen to being a suspected criminal locked in a cell facing a charge of murder.

***

My journey to the holding cell of a police station had started two days previously, early on Wednesday morning. I had rode to work with only an insurance claim for stolen goods to investigate; the insurers were deeply suspicious of the claimant's tale and I was assigned to discover the truth.

When I arrived at my office in Bridgeton, a woman in a business suit was standing outside my door staring at me with a look that was far from friendly.

She viewed me down the length of her nose, her face set in a furious frown.

"Good morning, can I help you?" I asked as I struggled to retrieve my keys from the pocket of my biker jacket.

"I take it you are Mr Campbell. You aren't very punctual, are you?" She sounded like someone who wasn't comfortable speaking to people below her social standing. My appearance meant she obviously felt that I was so far below her social status I was practically subterranean.

"That's me." I acknowledged both my name and her comment. I wasn't going to be fazed by her rude interruption to my morning routine.

The door swung open on my untidy little fiefdom. Her face folded into a shape that suggested further disapproval. She was already getting on my nerves.

"Please come in," I suggested. She entered but her reluctance was evident in her every movement.

I indicated the visitor's chair and she perched on it like she had been invited to sit on a bed of nails. I offered her tea or coffee as I removed my leathers. The sight of my Clash T-shirt and faded jeans did nothing to improve her opinion of me. She refused my offer of a beverage and also my suggestion that I should change into my office clothes. She was eager to conclude her business with me as quickly as possible.

I flopped down on my own side of the desk, determined to wind her up a little more if I could, although I did resist the urge to put my feet on the desk. "Now, how can I help you, Ms...?"

"My name is Nicole Chalmers, I work for the law firm of Boston and Unwin. One of our clients has asked us to contact you regarding a delicate matter." She spoke with polite formality reciting the introduction like she had rehearsed it; her accent was Scottish but she had chipped it away until it was almost undetectable. As she spoke, I studied her briefly and made a snapshot assessment. She was dressed in the type of stiff, navy blue suit that is supposed to help make women appear more powerful. It was strained across her bust and looked a little tight in other places. Below the suit, her expensive white silk blouse reflected the blue light of the sky coming in the window. Her light brown hair was styled severely, drawn back tightly from her face in a way that would flatter an older woman but looked too clinical on someone her age. A simple string of pearls hung around her neck, the only truly feminine touch to her starkly efficient city image. There was little make-up on her face, and the tired bags under her eyes told a story of a woman who had worked very hard to get to where she was. I imagined she was on course to make partner at her law firm before she was forty.

"And your client is?" I asked in reply to her statement.

"At the moment, that is not something you need to know. The only thing I can tell you is that discretion is of paramount importance in this matter and that we will not divulge the identity of our client until such times as you have been engaged on their behalf." I have never been very tolerant of the self-important, add it to my long list of flaws, but she was so far up her own backside I thought that I would need a proctologist just to communicate with her. She was really pressing every button and everything about her made me want to tell her to get out, but instead I had listened politely.

When she was finished I responded simply to her pomposity. "At the moment there is nothing you have said that makes me even vaguely interested in this, whatever it is." She was flustered slightly by my response but there was something about her that made me think she was used to getting her own way.

"What would you say if I told you that I was instructed to offer you twenty thousand pounds to take this case?" She looked smug.

'Oh ya beauty', I thought as I nearly fell off my wobbly old chair. I regained my composure and tried to pretend that people offered me a fortune every time they walked into my office.

"My first thought would be that you had managed to say something interesting. My second would be that you must be representing a seriously big-time criminal."

"I can assure you Mr Campbell, the person I represent is nothing of the sort. My client is in the entertainment industry and is keen to keep this affair out of the media." She bristled with haughty indignation.

"I'm sure that's how all the lawyers of the biggest gangsters would react." I threw out a hook and sure enough she bit, much to my amusement.

She looked even more flustered. "I can assure you that is not the case, you have my word on that." It was obvious that I had succeeded in disrupting her control of the situation but she believed that offering her word would put an end to any doubts I may have.

I refused to let her off the hook completely.

"Is there any chance that I will be asked to do anything criminal?"

"No, I don't believe so, it is simply evidence gathering. Now are you willing to take the case?" she asked forcefully, obviously annoyed at my obtuseness.

The truth was that my head was definitely turned and there were twenty thousand reasons it was spinning but I felt uncomfortable at the thought of working for someone I didn't know.

"I would need to meet the client," I said with as much authority as my diminished bank account would allow.

She looked at me as if she was staring over a poker hand. "I would have to consult my client about that. If you hear the basic details of what would be required, would that help?"

"Possibly," I replied.

"My client believes that his manager may be stealing money from him. It may be that the money is being used to pay debts the manager has or there could be any number of reasons. They have had a long-standing relationship and my client is concerned that if his suspicions prove to be unfounded, it would damage that relationship beyond repair. He requires you to gather evidence to either confirm or refute those suspicions."

"Why me?"

"Your recent exploits have attracted some publicity. My client has a good 'feeling' about you. He is a man who acts impulsively on his 'feelings'." She was referring to a couple of successful cases that I had worked previously. There was scorn in her voice which I was pretty sure would never be present when she spoke to her client. She was a woman who knew who was crucial in helping her climb up the precarious pole of promotion.

"Twenty thousand pounds is a lot to stake impulsively," I stated, while another side of me was screaming shut up and take the cash.

"As I said, he acts on his feelings. He believes that it has worked for him in his career up to now."

"Why does he think his manager is stealing from him now, if this is such a long relationship?"

"My client is a musician. The royalty cheques he receives from his manager have been diminishing despite the fact that his band's music was used in a recent Hollywood movie. Due to the exposure a film normally gives a band's songs, my client believes the cheques should be increasing. He is therefore concerned that his manager may be in some financial trouble. If that is the case it would be better that the relationship end quietly as he has no wish to involve the police. He feels that to do so would only make things worse for his long-time acquaintance."

I wondered if she was always so formal in the way she spoke. An image briefly crossed my mind of her telling her spouse that *'foreplay has reached the required number of minutes, you may now start copulation.'* It was not an image I wanted in my head for any length of time.

I concentrated on the matter in hand and considered what she had said. Although I understood the need for discretion, I felt that I would still require a meeting with any potential client.

"I would be willing to take this on, if your client agrees to a meeting. He can be assured that I would handle the matter tactfully, you have my word on that." I enjoyed throwing the phrase back at her.

"Fine, I will have to consult with him. Thank you for your time, Mr Campbell." She stood up briskly and offered her hand. I repeated the actions and she shook my hand with a limp gesture.

"I'll be in touch." She walked smartly to the door and out of the office.

***

About two hours later, as I sat with a long-lensed camera focused on the potential insurance fraudster, my mobile rang.

"Hello, Campbell Investigations, Craig Campbell speaking."

"Mr Campbell, Nicole Chalmers. I have spoken to my client, he has agreed to meet you tomorrow afternoon. I will e-mail you his address. I must request your utmost tact in this matter."

"Yes, Ms Chalmers, you have already stated that and I have already given you that assurance, you have my word. Will you be there tomorrow?"

"No, despite my advice he has decided to talk to you alone." She obviously felt that her client had lost his mind and that he could not be trusted to talk to the hired help.

"Is there anything else I should know before I go?"

"No, he will tell you the full story. Goodbye."

"Goodb..." The call had already been disconnected. I was positive that the fact Ms Chalmers' client had ignored her advice meant that she was a little annoyed at me.

The e-mail arrived about two minutes after the phone call was terminated. I was surprised to see that my prospective client was none other than Ben Jamieson, lead singer and songwriter with The Butterfly Collectors. They were a mid-nineties Scottish rock band who had achieved a good deal of success as part of the Brit-pop explosion. They had been among my favourite bands when I was at secondary school and I had been to see them live on a number of occasions.

If she had told me who the client was at the start I would have agreed to take the job right away.

As my surveillance target had been singularly unco-operative in his fraudulent behaviour, I decided to go home and listen to my old Butterfly Collectors CDs.

CHAPTER TWO

The gates were black, ten feet tall and tipped with gold spikes cast in the shape of the fleur de lis. They were an extremely attractive way to repel unwanted visitors. A plaque on one of the pillars read 'Carnation', the name of the house inspired by a song recorded by The Jam. I was sitting on the back of my brand new Ducati 1200s, my helmet resting on my lap.

The gates protected the Jamieson property that sat back from a sycamore-lined street in Newton Mearns. The affluent suburb lies to the south of the city and is home to a variety of professional people and wealthy citizens. I had been waiting for five minutes and was beginning to wonder if the occupants had forgotten about me when the intercom crackled.

"You can come in now," a woman's voice said.

The heavy gates began to swing open. Their movement was smooth and there was little sound from their thick hinges. There was some impressive engineering behind that simple action.

The gravel driveway snaked for about one hundred metres, the tall poplar trees providing shade from the sunlight. The drive ended in a substantial circular space. A sweep of the same yellow gravel surrounded both the house and a separate garage like a moat. There was an impressive rockery beyond the gravel and an extensive lawn beyond that stretched all the way to the fence at the front.

I parked at the doors of the modern four-car garage, beside a beautiful classic Harley Davidson motorcycle. I took a moment to admire the stylish American icon before I turned my attention to the house.

It was not the Georgian or Victorian stone villa I had been expecting. It was a brilliant white, art-deco design over two floors. There were curved bay windows lined with black metal, which separated the glass into small panes. The front door was recessed between the two curved rooms; it was painted in a striking black gloss with silver fittings that were contemporary with the rest of the building. I was about to knock when it swung away from me.

A beautiful girl in her late teens held the door open and looked at me like I was the tastiest dish on the menu.

"Mmm, you're a lot more handsome than I expected, I was expecting some old creep." She purred as she thrust a considerable cleavage in my direction.

"Thanks, but I'm not as handsome as I look. I've been enhanced in post-production," I responded, hoping that humour might divert her flirting.

She laughed, a trilling sound that exposed the young girl behind the woman's body.

"I'm Craig Campbell. I'm here to see Mr Jamieson."

"I know, silly. He's my dad." Her eyelids fluttered in time to her words.

My heart sank. This was not a good start. A hormonally challenged teenager might prove to be a problem, especially as she was the client's daughter.

"Is he around?"

"Yes, he's out on the tennis court with Mum. I'll take you to him." She wiggled her way through the house, glancing back to see if I was watching. I ignored her antics, embarrassed by her performance. She motioned me through a set of patio doors and back into the unseasonably warm autumnal sunshine.

On my left there was a glass-walled swimming pool connected to the main house by a short corridor. The court area was surrounded by a three-metre-high fence and lay behind the building that housed the pool. I thought about how I had contributed to the opulence on show by purchasing those CDs and buying my concert tickets.

I walked to the edge of the fence that surrounded a blue and white tennis court. On one side of the net was Ben Jamieson, looking much as I remembered him. His shoulder-length blonde hair was darkened by sweat, clinging to his face. That face was glowing with a healthy tan, and the thin crow's feet that radiated from the edges of his blue eyes appeared to be the only sign that he was now in his forties. What I could see of his bony frame was a nut-brown colour, with no sign of any fat. His infamous excesses of the nineties did not seem to have done him much harm. His clothes would not have been welcome within the confines of Wimbledon but judging by his tennis game, that was never going to be something he would have to worry about. He wore a black T-shirt with The Jam band logo on it, bright green Hawaiian shorts and a pair of luminous yellow trainers. He was unlikely to be voted GQ's fashion icon of the year.

His opponent was his wife, Lisa. She was the main donor of the attractive genes her daughter had inherited, although the young woman had her father's blonde hair. Lisa was dark-haired with a naturally olive skin that made her look as if she was a native of a country on the Mediterranean coast. I knew her background was a little more mundane - she came from somewhere in the Midlands. She was dressed in proper tennis attire, pale blue shirt and shorts with white trainers. She also looked fit and healthy, a woman in the prime of her life.

"Dad, it's the private detective guy."

He acknowledged me, "Oh. how you doin'? We'll just finish this game, OK? Thirty-love."

I felt a little irritated by the delay but I had twenty

thousand reasons to keep my vexation to myself.

Lisa was serving and was apparently the more accomplished player of the two. She won the next two points with rasping forehand drives that left her husband flat-footed and defeated.

When the game was over they picked up towels and wiped away the visible sign of their exertions.

Ben walked towards me and offered his hand. "Ben Jamieson, thanks for comin', this is Lisa and ye've met Carla." His smile was warm and genuine and I witnessed at first hand the charisma that had helped to make him a star.

"Hello, sorry for interrupting your game," I replied while addressing Lisa.

"Nae worries, she always wins anyway, she's the real player. Ah just dae it tae get some exercise. Better than being stuck in the gym, bores the arse aff me that place." His accent had not changed since his days as a kid in Easterhouse.

"I just do a bit of running, no real sporting skills I'm afraid," I returned.

He laughed at his own lack of skill. "Neither huv ah, ye've seen me play."

After she had towelled away her sweat, Lisa approached me. I shook her hand and she gestured to a table and chairs on some decking close to the house. "Shall we take a seat?"

We walked in a group towards the decking, where Carla had settled on a sun lounger, listening to her iPod on a pair of expensive headphones. Her interest in me seemed to have waned already, much to my relief.

As I sat at the table a middle-aged woman appeared from the house bearing a tray. She deposited a jug of lemonade, some fresh fruit and glasses on the table.

"Thanks, Marie," Lisa said.

Ben poured the lemonade for each of us and settled into his chair.

"So you met Nicole, auld frigid knickers?" he asked with a mischievous smile.

"Eh, yes."

"She's a cracker isn't she? Ah've made it a life ambition tae make her laugh but ah've no managed it yet." His smile became a grin, the look of a mischievous kid planning a prank.

"She told me about your concerns about your manager."

"Aye, she didnae want me to be involved personally but ah think ah need tae. Ah've known Kris a long time."

"Tell me about him."

He became more serious. "Kris wis the band's first and only manager. He helped us get signed, he stuck wi' me efter the band split. He's been good fur ma career. Ah widnae say we wur pals but he's always looked efter me."

"So what's changed to make you suspect him?"

His mood dampened further. "Nicole probably told ye that oor music wiz used in a film at the start o' the year. The guys an' me have been offered a reunion tour on the back o' it. But the money we've been gettin' fae royalties has actually went doon. It looks like it's confirmed whit the rest o' the guys always thought. They fell out wi' Kris long afore the band split. They thought he wis stealin' fae us back then but ah didnae believe it. Ah'm beginning tae wonder if he's taking mair than his fair share and that they were right aw alang."

"Why not go to the police? I don't see a problem if he's not a friend."

He shook his head. "Naw, he's done a lot fur me. Ah jist want tae know if he's takin' the cash, that's aw. If you find oot that he is, then ah'll huv a think aboot whit tae dae next. But ah cannae get the polis involved withoot any proof."

I turned to Lisa. "What do you think?"

"Personally, I think he's a crook and that you're right, the police are the best option but it's Ben's decision," she said loyally.

"The money you're offering me, it's a lot more than I would normally get," I said to Ben.

"Look, man, ah've goat money. Ah need this tae be done wi' nae fuss. Fae what ah've read aboot ye, you're a man o' integrity. Ah'm payin' fur that integrity, no fur whit ye'll dae. There's plenty o' guys ah came across in the music industry wi fuck aw integrity and money wiz aw they wur interested in."

"Thanks but you're taking a risk on me, after all you don't know me." I tried to play devil's advocate even with the knowledge that my bank manager would disagree.

He cracked one of his trademark smiles. "Let's just say ah've goat a gut feelin' about ye." I thought of Nicole's disdain for Ben's gut feelings.

I wasn't sure what to say. Twenty grand would pay my bills for a few months and maybe let me get out of the insurance investigation business altogether but it also was a heavy responsibility. I weighed the pros and cons and decided that if I could help a boyhood hero and make some cash then it was a good thing. If it had been anyone else I would probably have turned them down but he was very persuasive and it was an opportunity to give me some financial security at least for a short time.

"OK, I'll take the job but you need to let me do it my way. It might mean wandering along the lines of what's legal, so the less you know the better, just in case I cross that line."

"Sure, nae problem but ah don't want ye daein' anythin' that might get ye intae bother with the bizzies. Dae whit ye kin and let me know how ye get oan."

"I'll need your manager's details."

"Carla." He shouted at his daughter before waving his hands to attract her attention.

"What?" she sighed.

"Would ye get ma phone fae the games room, please?"

"Christ." She threw the headphones down on the lounger and stormed into the house.

"Teenagers." Ben was embarrassed but not enough to rebuke her. I didn't see him as a strict disciplinarian.

She returned and gave her father his phone. He asked for my mobile number and texted me the address of Kris McAvoy, his manager. He then asked for my bank account details and arranged the payment with his accountant as I waited.

As we walked back through the house on my way out he asked me, "Did ye like the band?"

"Aye, I was a big fan." I admitted.

"Did you ever read oor biography?"

"No, I never got round to it."

"Ah don't think many did. Wait there I'll get you a copy. Ah've still goat hunners." He grinned again and went upstairs. He returned with the book which had been written by a journalist called Rebecca Marsh.

"It's signed, might be worth somethin' when ah'm deid." He laughed and handed the hardback to me.

"Whit's yir bike?" he asked as indicated my helmet.

"Oh, a Ducati 1200s"

"D'ye mind if ah take a look?"

"No, be my guest." He followed me out to the garage and sat on the bike. I inserted the key and pressed the starter. I could see his boyish pleasure on his face as he revved the engine.

"Nice pipes," he said after he had turned off the considerable noise.

"Your bike's pretty special," I said with genuine admiration.

"It's a 1971 Hydraglide. Ah found it on a website. It was in some mess but ah restored it. Took me six months but it looks good noo, d'ye think?"

"Definitely."

"Want a go?"

"No thanks. I'd love to but I better be going."

"OK man. You need anythin' let me know and if ye change yir mind about the bike just gie's a bell."

"Cheers. I'll be in touch."

He stood beside the Harley as I rode back down the drive.

As I exited, I noticed a young man dressed in an old sixties parka sitting against the fence outside the gates. He was wearing a vacant look as if his mind was somewhere else. He was so distant that I thought that he might be on something. He was pouring a hot drink from a flask and organising sandwiches. It looked like he was settling down for the day, in the hope he would see his musical hero. I wondered how anyone could be so obsessed by a band or a singer that they would take up residence outside their house. It was none of my business so I turned the bike into the road and headed for home.

CHAPTER THREE

I rode back across the Kingston Bridge to Carol's flat at Glasgow Harbour. I had moved in with her two months previously when the lease on my flat expired. Although being with Carol was great, I missed the character of my old place.

As the time came for Carol to come home from work, I cooked some risotto and set the table.

She looked tired when she walked in but was keen to hear about my day. "Well how did it go with your rock star? Were you all star-struck then?

"No, as a matter of fact, I was professional and cool. Although I was a bit unnerved by his teenage daughter who seems to think she's a sex kitten," I confessed.

"Oh yes? Tell me more." She smiled, enjoying my discomfort.

"Let's just say that she was less than subtle at her attempts to attract my attention."

Her smile widened to a grin. "Craig's got a fan, who knew?"

"Hey, don't say it as if it's a great surprise."

"Aw, did I hurt my darling's feelings?" She ruffled my hair as if I was six years old.

"Stop that." I laughed and wrestled her into an embrace that led to a kiss.

"What's for dinner? I'm starving," she said as she walked to the bedroom to get changed.

I told her and she voiced her approval.

We ate the risotto and enjoyed a glass of pinot grigio to wash it down.

***

As it was Thursday, it was pub quiz night, the one night a week that I spent in the company of my mates Li, Barry and Paul.

The walk to the pub was a bit longer than it used to be but it meant I got some exercise before the night's indulgences.

On the way, my phone dinged to tell me that I had received a text. I didn't recognise the number but it didn't take me long to realise who it was from.

'Nce mtng u 2day. We shld get together sometime. Carla."

I groaned. My belief that she had forgotten about me was a little optimistic. Discretion being the better part of valour, I ignored it.

I was the first to arrive and chatted briefly with Brenda, The Auld Tavern's manager and best barmaid. She had recently divorced from her husband and some of the light and humour she brought to the bar had diminished a little. Our conversation was brief and trivial. I paid for our round and took the tray with the drinks to a table just as Barry and Paul arrived.

They settled in to their chairs and we began our review of the week. When it was my turn and I told them about Jamieson, I could see their eyes light up. Ever since my job had included murder and kidnap, their interest in what I had to say had increased considerably. The details of insurance fraud never held as much attraction for them for some reason.

"Ben Jamieson, lead singer with The Butterfly Collectors, really?" Paul asked.

"Yip. I can't tell you what he needs me for but I was at his house out in Newton Mearns this afternoon."

"Oh hark at you, hobnobbing with celebrities. What's he like?" Barry joined the discussion.

"He's all right. Seems like an ordinary guy. Well an ordinary guy that's made a mint."

"Did you talk about the band? Are they going to do the reunion tour?" It was Paul's turn to continue the interrogation.

"It's a bit up in the air at the moment due to what I've been asked to help him with."

My best mate Li arrived to complete our regular

team line-up. Before I got a chance to tell him, Paul said, "Guess who Inspector Morse here is working for now?"

"Don't tell me he's got the job of finding ze Pink Panther diamond?" Li said with a crap French accent and his characteristic irreverent smile.

The others laughed and Barry said, "Aye, you're right enough. He is more like Inspector Clouseau than Morse."

There was more hilarity at my expense before I finally told Li about my new client.

"Wow, detective to the stars. You're moving up in the world Campbell. What's it all about then? His wife been getting some extra-marital attention by shagging the help?"

"It's not that but I'm not at liberty to say. Client confidentiality."

"Bollocks." Li just laughed. There was never any chance of my head staying in the clouds too long, I could always rely on the three of them to keep me grounded.

The quiz master called the evening to order and we started our pursuit of the £100 cash prize. By half-time we were well placed in third and even had a chance to win. Li went to get the next round of drinks in and Paul had gone to the toilet.

"Barry, I need to try to get some evidence from a computer, discreetly. Do you have anything that might help?" I was hoping that Barry's prowess with computers and the range of tools he had at his disposal would give me a way to do some digging into McAvoy's recent behaviour.

"If you can get temporary access, then yes. I've got a program that will copy a complete image of a PC to one of my servers and you can look at what's on it from there. But it would be highly illegal," he warned.

"I guessed that would be the case but my plan would be to check it, write a report and then delete the image."

"Look mate, I can make it secure but if anyone finds out I'll be in prison with you." He looked a little concerned.

"I don't want to get you into hot water, Barry. Can you send it somewhere else? Another server maybe?"

"There might be a way. I'll make a few calls and ring you tomorrow."

"Cheers, thanks."

The others rejoined us just in time for the second half of the quiz. We performed quite well and finished the night in second spot, which meant we celebrated a £20 prize by buying another round with some snacks. We love to live at the cutting edge of the rock 'n' roll lifestyle.

***

Carol was asleep when I returned to the flat, so I brewed a strong Costa Rican coffee and settled down with a mug and the book that Ben had given me. The title came from one of the band's biggest hits. The writer's name was Rebecca Marsh, she had been the music correspondent for one of the Scottish broadsheets back in the nineties. She became an author and had written three biographies about Scottish celebrities since 2005.

Passion and poise:
The Butterfly Collectors Story

Beginnings

Many people wonder what music would have been like if Elvis Presley hadn't walked into Sun Records and met Sam Phillips. How different would the world have been if Paul McCartney hadn't gone to a summer fete to see a band called The Quarrymen and their captivating leader, John Lennon?

Like most great things in music, The Butterfly Collectors would not have existed without the intervention of fate, or kismet, or destiny, or whatever you would like to call it.

If Ben Jamieson hadn't been placed in the same class as Jim Harris at the start of their third year at St Dominic's High School, there might not have been five albums and seven number one hits from one of Scotland's most successful rock acts.

Ben Jamieson was born on 13th August, 1971 at the Glasgow Royal Maternity Hospital, known to all Glaswegians as the Rottenrow. He was the third of five children to Davie and Agnes Jamieson.

A restless child, his only passion was for music from an early age. His father introduced him to The Beatles, The Stones and all the giants of rock by playing his large collection of albums and talking passionately to his son about each of the bands. He was further exposed to the rock classics as his mum loved the smooth sound of The Eagles and James Taylor. While his brothers and sisters were outside playing games, Ben would sit with his Dad's headphones connected to the family stereo, lyrics sheets and album covers clutched in his hands.

The young Jamieson would entertain his family with his own interpretations of the songs that he loved from his parents' albums. His impression of Mick Jagger singing "Let's Spend The Night Together" was requested at every family gathering as he pranced and preened in a passable imitation of his hero. He would never be shy about expressing himself in a performance.

Davie bought his son his first guitar when he was eight but Ben struggled to get to grips with the instrument. He couldn't make his chubby fingers do what was required and after a frustrating twelve months he gave up. His dad was very supportive and he continued to encourage young Ben at every opportunity. He put a little money away to get his music-loving boy an electronic keyboard for Christmas. Ben's fingers still lacked the necessary dexterity to play the instrument well but he could at least produce a tune.

By 1981, as the new electronic music began to replace British Punk and the American New Wave, Ben was composing his own songs, picking the notes out on the keyboard and writing simplistic lyrics.

He wanted to write songs like his new hero Paul Weller but at ten years old his talent was raw and a long way from the skills of The Jam's frontman. There was never any chance of him letting anyone hear these early attempts but they were valuable lessons that would help him to become the band's key songwriter.

He hated the new sounds that were filling the charts from bands like the Human League and Depeche Mode. His heroes played in bands with guitars and he was annoyed at his own inability to play the instrument that is the very essence of rock.

As he reached the age to attend secondary school, he continued to write but it was in isolation. His mates would still rather kick a ball than listen to a new album or pick up an instrument. He wasn't great academically, although he did enjoy music and English at which he excelled. The other subjects held no interest for him and he was disruptive in most of his classes, earning the enmity of his teachers and many of his classmates.

One of his teachers, Gordon Bellamy, remembered how difficult it was to get Ben to focus. "He was a constant challenge as he seemed incapable of sitting still. I would find his jotters filled with lyrics and ideas for stories but little of the geography I was supposed to be teaching him."

He began his third year at secondary school with little prospect of earning much in the way of academic qualifications. On the first day, in the English class, he sat next to a boy called Jim Harris.

It took Jim Harris a little longer than Ben to become a music fan. A visit to one of his cousins when he was ten was the catalyst. His cousin, Graham, was a big fan of the Ramones and Blondie. Graham played 'End Of The Century', the Ramones fourth studio album to Jim. The younger cousin was immediately captivated and within months had managed to build an impressive collection of second-hand singles and albums. He would listen to anything and had an almost compulsive need to discover music that was new to him. He traced the roots of rock back through Led Zeppelin, The Beatles and Elvis. Eventually he began buying up collections of the blues masters like BB King, Muddy Waters and Robert Johnson. He was addicted to music.

At school Jim was a quiet lad, intense and permanently scruffy. He had avoided Ben before that meeting in the English class as he felt Jamieson was a troublemaker.

When Jim sat beside him that day, Ben noticed that the school bag Jim carried was covered in badges, all of them bearing the logo of a band. A

Led Zeppelin pin sat comfortably beside The Jam and Ramones. Ben had found a kindred spirit and began to ask Jim about the music he liked.

Jim's passion was for anything with a guitar and they began to build a friendship filled with the exchange of mix tapes and visits to record stores. They introduced each other to new bands and classic bands they hadn't listened to before. It provided the basis of all that was to follow both musically and in their friendship.

My eyelids began to droop and despite the coffee, sleep was winning. I put the book down and went to bed with Ramones songs rolling round my head.

CHAPTER FOUR

Barry was as good as his word and rang me at ten the following morning to say that he had something for me.

I met him at lunchtime in Kelvingrove Park, close to the university where he worked. He looked a little apprehensive as he approached the bench I was sitting on. It was like we were cold war spies in a Le Carré novel and I almost burst out laughing at our antics.

"Hi Barry, thanks for this, I appreciate it."

He reached into a pocket and handed me a USB flash drive.

"It's pretty simple. Plug it into the computer and as long as it's a standard PC the program will run automatically. It will install on to the hard drive and then delete itself from the USB drive. The main program will work in the background, set up a secure network connection to the server and then create a mirror image of the computer. It's a one time deal, it deletes from the hard drive as soon as the image has been copied."

"What about the server?"

"It belongs to a guy I know in the hacker community. He's cool and won't look at anything you do. If I'm being honest, it's probably more secure than a lot of corporate servers. Just make sure you delete the image when you're done." He stressed the importance of this by both the look on his face and the tone of his voice.

"How do I get to the data?"

"Give me a ring when it's done and I'll help you out."

"Thanks mate. I'm sorry for dragging you into this but I don't know how else I would go about it."

"OK but you didn't get this from me." He cracked a strained smile.

"I know."

"Oh, if the copy is interrupted, you're stuffed. The program will delete itself on reboot."

"I understand."

He stood up and we exchanged farewells.

***

Now that I had the means to harvest the information, I had to engineer an opportunity to meet Kris McAvoy and find out if he was stealing from Ben and how much.

I occasionally used an alias when I worked on insurance fraud. Among my deceitful business cards was solicitor Leonard Turner. Leonard was a useful character because despite their reputation, people still have a level of trust in lawyers.

I jumped on the bike and went back to Carol's flat. For some reason I couldn't explain, I couldn't quite bring myself to think of it as our flat, not yet, anyway.

I phoned McAvoy's office. "Good afternoon, McAvoy Agency, Sandra speaking. How may I help you?"

"Good afternoon, Sandra. My name is Leonard Turner. I was wondering if I could make an appointment to meet Mr McAvoy."

"Can I ask what it is regarding?"

"It is a delicate matter that I have been requested by my clients to handle on their behalf. I am a contract lawyer acting for a rock band who are thinking of changing agents and they would like me to speak to Mr McAvoy."

"One moment, please."

There was a brief hiatus before she said, "Mr Turner, can you come to our offices today?"

"Certainly. What time?"

"Mr McAvoy will be available from three."

"That's fine. I'll see you then."

***

I put on my crispest shirt under my sharpest suit, adorned it with my smartest tie and my shini-

41

est cufflinks. The disguise was rounded off with my polished black shoes accompanied by a slightly beat-up briefcase. I combed my unruly hair into something that approached respectability. I coaxed the normally unmanageable mess into place with the aid of some of Carol's hair products from the bathroom cabinet. I looked in the mirror and thought I could pass as a successful lawyer.

I picked out a Mont Blanc pen that I had been given as a graduation present and put it in the case with a collection of random bits of paper. I slipped the book that Jamieson had given me into the briefcase to help me to occupy some time if my plan went as I hoped.

I decided that the underground railway would be a better choice for my solicitor persona than my Ducati. I walked to Partick station and bought a ticket for the "Clockwork Orange" as the system is affectionately known by Glaswegians. I alighted at Buchanan Street with plenty of time before my meeting, which gave me the excuse to go for a strong coffee. One cappuccino later I was walking to the agency office.

McAvoy's offices were in the heart of Glasgow city centre, in a red sandstone Victorian block on St Vincent Street. The imposing building was a reminder of when Glasgow was the second city of the British Empire, a celebration of the city's commercial success of the nineteenth century.

After a climb of three flights of stairs, I reached my goal. A simple polished brass plaque indicated the McAvoy Agency on a plain wooden door with a frosted glass window. I walked into an office with four modern desks. Two women and one man were working at their respective computers. On the white-painted walls were photographs of various bands and a number of gold records glittering and proclaiming the success of McAvoy's charges.

A young woman with black hair was the first to acknowledge me. "Can I help you?" she asked with a pleasant smile.

"My name is Leonard Turner, I have an appointment with Mr McAvoy." Leonard is a quietly spoken man with a humble attitude.

An older woman, who looked to be in her early forties came from behind her desk. She was dressed in an understated black business suit with a close-fitting skirt. She walked with a straight back, poised and graceful, her four-inch high heels helping to give her an arresting air.

"Mr Turner, I'm Sandra Brown, Mr McAvoy's personal assistant. I'll take you through." She indicated a door at the end of the room.

She radiated a calm efficiency as she led me into a spacious office with large windows that looked out on to the bustle of St Vincent Street three floors below. To my right, the wall was dominated by a large corporate artwork that would have made my stomach churn and my head ache if I had to stare at it all day. In the corner, in front of the window was a glass-topped desk and behind it sat Kris McAvoy.

"Mr McAvoy, this is Mr Turner."

McAvoy stood up and offered me a welcoming grin and large hand. "Please call me Kris."

"Leonard," I said as he gripped my palm with the strength of a gorilla. I tried to return the challenge.

"Would you like something to drink Leonard?" he asked.

"A glass of water would be fine, thank you."

"Could you organise that please, Sandra?"

"Certainly, do you want anything?"

He thought for a second before asking for a peppermint tea. She walked away briskly to organise the drinks.

Kris McAvoy was from the same generation as Ben Jamieson. His fair hair was shoulder length, his face covered in a well-trimmed designer stubble. His face was tanned and shone as if he used plenty of moisturiser. His smile seemed genuine but there was something in his steel-grey eyes that hinted at a life that wasn't quite as wonderful as he would have me believe. It was the appearance of confidence rather than the genuine article.

He was dressed in an immaculate light grey suit, which looked to be of Italian cut and finish. A pale yellow shirt and grey tie all added to the illusion of confidence he was projecting.

His speech was more refined Glasgow businessman

than the working class chancer he had started his working life as.

Sandra delivered the water in a jug with ice and slices of lemon, as well as the tea for McAvoy.

"Now I believe I might be able to help you, is that correct Leonard?"

"Well Kris, not so much me as my clients," I said humbly.

"Tell me more," he said enthusiastically.

I feigned an apologetic tone. "I'm afraid at this moment I'm not at liberty to say who our clients are. They are a successful rock band who are dissatisfied with their current management arrangements. They have asked my firm to tactfully sound out some other agents around the country." I reflected on the irony of me sounding much like Nicole Chambers had in my office.

He nodded as I spoke with his hands in the position of prayer in front of his face. "Yes, I understand. What is the nature of their dissatisfaction?"

"It's all a bit tense at the moment. They believe that the agency in question took advantage of them when they started out and they would prefer not to continue with an arrangement that appears to give the band less than they believe they deserve."

He nodded constantly as I spun my story.

"Yes, it's a familiar story in our business I'm afraid. So what exactly would you like me to do?" There seemed to be no embarrassment or sense of irony in his words.

"Although I realise that every client is different, I was hoping you could show me one of your standard contracts for me to go over with the band. It would give them some idea of what is available." I thought I was doing well for someone who had no real idea what he was talking about.

"It's a bit unusual and of course every artist has different needs and demands but I suppose we could do that."

He walked to the door and as he did I palmed the flash drive from my pocket.

"Sandra, can I get a copy of the standard contract for established artists?" he asked as he walked out of the room.

I dropped some of the papers and my expensive pen on the floor and made sure they went in the direction of the computer that was suspended in a mount under his desk. I bent to pick up the papers and slipped the drive into one of the USB slots and pushed the pen out of sight under the computer. I planned to use the pen as an excuse to return later to retrieve the flash drive. I was getting back to my seat just as he came back into the room with a document in his hand.

"Are you OK?"

"I'm fine, sorry, I just dropped these papers, I've always been a little clumsy." I tried to look flustered and blushed in shame.

"Here it is, this is our standard contract. There are

different clauses added to suit the needs of individual clients but this should give you an idea of what we do."

I took the document from him, gave it a cursory glance before putting it inside the briefcase.

"Is there anything else I can help you with?"

"Can I ask you, is it very exciting working in the music business?"

"It has its good moments and its challenges, as you must know."

"Oh, no, not me. This is the first time I've had any dealings with any musical artist. It's normally our main office in London that deals with this kind of work but the band members have asked us to look all around the UK for a new management team to look after them."

"It must be a bit different for you, more interesting than what you are used to?" He was making polite noises as I twittered on.

"Oh, yes. Quite exciting really. How many acts do you look after?" I sounded as if I was a little star-struck.

"We have twenty two on the books at the moment. Some are brand new, just starting out really. Others have been with us for a long time. It's constantly changing as people's musical taste changes. You need to stay ahead of the game."

"You were the manager of The Butterfly Collectors at one time, is that right?"

"Aye, they were my very first. We were good for each other. I still look after Ben Jamieson, the lead singer." His smile appeared genuine as if he was remembering his early days in the business with a fondness that was no longer there.

"Yes, I remember them. They were very good. I'll not delay you any longer, thank you for your time. I will be visiting a few more agencies in Scotland and then I will report back to the band but you've been very helpful."

"You're welcome and I hope we'll be able to do business very soon."

"I certainly hope so." We exchanged another manly handshake and I left the office.

I took a long breath of relief as I walked down the stairs. This criminal enterprise felt like more excitement than I could bear. When I was out of sight of the office I ruffled my hair and loosened my constricting tie.

***

My plan was to return to their office later that day with the intention of getting the flash drive and the pen. I hoped that the boss would have gone by the time I arrived and that I might get the staff talking.

I phoned Carol and told her that I might be a bit late and that I would get something to eat when I came home.

In yet another coffee franchise, I ordered a latte

and a muffin. I sat on a comfortable armchair at the window and lifted The Butterfly Collectors biography from my briefcase. I flicked through until I found the part about how McAvoy became the band's manager.

On The Up

Jim Harris was getting dispirited by the band's lack of progress in finding a record deal. Despite positive feedback from audiences and even the support of a local radio DJ, no A&R man was willing to take a chance on them. Guitar bands had been having a hard time of it since the rise of dance music in the late eighties.

His frustration reached a peak at a band meeting on 12th April 1991, and he told the others that he wanted to quit. Ben was shocked and pleaded with Jim to reconsider. Mark was inclined to agree with Jim. The band was his only source of income and he was coming under increasing pressure from his parents to get a "real job". Kenny worked part-time in a warehouse and he was willing to keep gigging as he thought of their music as a bit of fun that earned him some extra spending money.

Ben took the floor and argued his case forcefully. "The first thing we need to do is find a manager. It's important that we take this seriously. We need to be more professional."

Jim was quick to reply. "Christ, we've got no money now, how the hell are we going to afford a manager?"

"We make sure he or she only gets money as a percentage of what we make, at least at first. That way they have to do the work to help us make more money. If we can get better bookings maybe the record companies will finally take some notice." Ben was as passionate and optimistic about the band as ever and was dismayed at the thought of it all falling apart. Music was his life and he had no idea what he could do if he wasn't in the band. He had no qualifications and no wish to have any other career.

"We've got three gigs in May and June, if we can't find anyone by then we review it and make a decision," Ben argued.

"Fine by me, if nothing happens by then I'll be off." Mark showed that he was willing to try one last time.

With the other three still keen to keep going, Jim relented and agreed to Ben's proposal but his natural pessimism meant he wasn't as confident as their frontman.

The first gig after the meeting was scheduled to be held in King Tut's Wah Wah Hut in Glasgow's St Vincent Street. It had opened the previous year and with a three hundred capacity was becoming one of the best small venues in the city. Such was its growing reputation, the band were genuinely excited to be playing there.

The crowd was enthusiastic and supportive as the lights came up and Jim struck the first chord. The tiny stage, at the rear of the old building, left little room for Ben to perform his usual acrobatic and athletic antics. The lack of space did seem to help them focus and they played better than ever with a set that included some original songs as well as some cover versions of classic tracks. Ben's magnetic persona captivated an audience that was made up of confirmed fans of the band in conjunction with the Hut's regulars and the musically curious, and the cheers and applause grew with every song.

Among the regular patrons was Kris McAvoy. McAvoy had bought into the age of entrepreneurship in a big way. He left school on the day he turned sixteen and had spent the four years since trying to find ways to make his fortune. Some of those methods bordered on the illegal and some of them waved the border good-bye, looking over their shoulder with not a care in the world. He spent his weekends at the famous Barras market selling pirate videos while being vigilant for the police raids that occasionally disrupted trade in Glasgow's East End.

One of his friends had suggested that there was money to be made in music management if he could find the right band. Ever since the idea was suggested to him he had spent a lot of time in King Tut's and other venues listening to the decent, the dreadful and the ugly. The night The Butterfly Collectors played he knew his persistence had paid off as the audience reaction made him believe that he had found the band he was looking for.

The guys were buzzing after the performance

and joined the crowd in the bar at the front of the building. They sat chatting excitedly about the set when a skinny blond-haired guy in a suit that looked two sizes too big for him walked towards them.

"Hi lads, I'm Kris McAvoy and I'm going to make you famous." He spoke with an unshakeable confidence that defied his lack of experience or knowledge.

There was general hilarity among the band. This cocky little man didn't look like he was their manager in waiting, more like one of the spivs who would sell knock-off merchandise outside a concert.

"Laugh if you like boys but I'll prove it to you." He felt a little hurt at their first reaction but he was determined to prove them wrong. It was a determination that was to be a repeating theme during their time together.

He walked away and the band went back to drinking and signing autographs for some of their fans. In the days after the gig they forgot all about McAvoy's boast.

One week later, the next gig was at Nice 'n' Sleazy in Sauchiehall Street. Another storming set had further energised the band and as they were packing up the same blond guy in the same suit appeared, shoulders set and huge grin decorating his face.

"God, look it's Brian Epstein," Kenny mocked.

"I'm going to be your manager and to prove it I've got this." McAvoy boldly thrust a poster towards the group. It contained professionally produced *graphics and included a new logo for the band. At the bottom were twelve dates in August and September of that year for venues across Scotland and the North of England.*

Ben was impressed by the quality of the artwork but was more than a little cynical. "A very nice poster, pal, but what does that prove? Anybody can get posters made."

McAvoy refused to back down. "First, I've seen your posters and they're shite. Second, these are confirmed dates, if you don't want them I'll find somebody that does."

His accurate comment regarding their posters provoked a laugh from each of the band members.

"What, you arranged this in a week?" Jim was incredulous.

"Yep. So you interested or not?" He had pulled a lot of strings to arrange everything and was now desperately hoping that he had secured the right to manage them.

"You've got some balls, pal." Ben laughed and shook his head. "We better sit and have a talk then Mr Manager."

The others were a little more hesitant but two hours later they had shaken hands on a deal with the bold little man in his Dad's suit.

The third gig at the beginning of June was their best yet and the positive feeling among the band members was increased when Ben wrote four new songs in July for their first real tour. There was a new energy about the songs, a new sense of hope that defined a new mood.

I finished reading at that point. I considered the strange ability of McAvoy to secure those gigs in such a short time. How did he achieve that much in a week? Maybe he was a talented salesman but I thought there was something not altogether straight-forward about it.

***

At quarter to six the staff of the coffee shop were lifting upturned chairs on to tables and mopping the floor around me. I took the hint and walked out into the soft drizzling rain.

I was back at the McAvoy office five minutes later. I opened the outer door but the staff had already gone home. I could see a light shining through in the space between the frame and the door of McAvoy's office.

I would have to get the pen, make my apologies to McAvoy and leave. If I got the chance I would retrieve the flash drive, but I wasn't optimistic.

I knocked on the door but there was no reply. When I tried the handle and found it unlocked, I quickly realised why there had been no reply.

McAvoy was sitting on his chair, his head lolling to one side. There was a black circular hole in the middle of his forehead with a small red line of blood tracing a path to his nose. The hole looked like a macabre Hindu decoration. His eyes stared blankly at the ceiling, as if he was deep in thought. The hole in the window behind him radiated a web of cracks, the glass spotted with blood, shards of bone and pieces of flesh and brain.

I stood for a moment mesmerised by the pattern of the cracks, my eyes fixed on anything other than the evidence of a life extinguished. I had to shake myself out of the torpor brought on by my mental and physical shock.

I gulped in a breath and shuddered as I bent to retrieve the flash drive. I attached it to my key ring and went back into the outer office. I sat on the edge of the P.A.'s desk and dialled 999.

"Emergency services, which service do you require?"

"Police. I'd like to report a murder."

CHAPTER FIVE

Half an hour later I was sitting in McAvoy's outer office with a glass of water, which I was using to wash away the acrid, acidic taste of bile. The police had begun to arrive ten minutes after I called, strobing the street below with blue flashing lights. Two uniformed officers were first on the scene followed by their detective colleagues fifteen minutes later. The younger of the two constables had followed the same path I had taken to the toilet. His partner smiled sympathetically at his youthful colleague's reaction. He had probably reacted in a similar way at some time in the past.

The senior constable took a brief statement from me about how I had discovered the body. His questions were brief, laying the groundwork for the more detailed probing by the detectives that would follow. The news that I was a private investigator was greeted less than enthusiastically. The revelations about the News Of The World's pet phone tapper had lowered the opinion of the whole country against a trade that was already looked on as a shower of amoral opportunists. There would be little point in me arguing that I was a different animal.

The uniformed officers seemed happy to accept my story at face value but I knew there were awkward questions that would prove difficult to answer if someone thought to ask them.

The first detective to speak to me was a Detective Sergeant from 'A' Division. His name was Mark Burton, a thirty-something string bean of a man, six feet five inches tall with not a trace of excess flesh to be seen. He had ice-blue eyes separated by a long, pointed nose and underlined by a sliver of a mouth, all set on a long oval face. He spoke quietly, paused after every answer I offered and unnerved me with his slightly odd, very slow way of speaking.

"Mr Campbell, I think you should tell me what happened to bring us to this point," he said with a protracted precise enunciation as he fidgeted with his pen.

"I was hired by a client to investigate Mr McAvoy. My client, Ben Jamieson..."

"The Butterfly Collectors singer?" he interrupted.

"Yes, that's right. He hired me to find out if Mr McAvoy was stealing from him. I came here on a pretence earlier this afternoon and left a pen. I was hoping to use it as an excuse to come back this evening and get a look around his office or to talk to one of the staff when their boss wasn't around." I had no intention of telling him about the flash drive, not just for my sake but to ensure that Barry would not be sucked in to the mire in which I now found myself.

"You do know that searching an empty office would have been illegal, right?" His deliberate, whispered delivery was worse than anyone screaming at me. It grated on my nerves and put me on edge.

"Yes, as I said, I was hoping that I could get the proof of McAvoy's guilt or innocence by speaking to the staff. If I discovered anything I was going to give it to Mr Jamieson and he could decide what to do about it."

"Yes... but if the office is empty, it would still have been illegal. Why didn't Mr Jamieson come to us?"

"He felt that he owed Mr McAvoy something for all that he did for him and his band." I didn't think there was any point in highlighting the fact that the office would have been locked if there was no one here; he was supposed to be the detective.

"Why didn't you come to us?" he pressed.

"I understood and respected his reasons for keeping it quiet until he had proof of his suspicions. There may have been nothing to his fears so there was no point in getting the police involved until we were sure."

"What did you see when you came back?"

"The outer office door was open and there was no

one in the room, I noticed that there was a light on in Mr McAvoy's office. I was expecting to have to apologise to Mr McAvoy, collect my pen and find another way to gather the information. When I opened the door I discovered his body. Then I called you."

"Where's this pen you were meant to be coming back for?"

"It should still be under his desk, unless he found it and picked it up."

"Have you washed your hands since you called us?"

I was puzzled by his change of subject but said, "Yes, after I called you I was sick in the toilet. It's the first time I've seen the contents of anyone's head and it was a bit of a shock, to say the least. I washed my hands after that."

"OK. You'll have to come to the station to make a statement."

"I understand."

He wrote some more notes and folded his notebook which he put in the top pocket of his jacket. He walked away without another word, his arms swinging like skinny pendulums by his side.

As the crime scene technicians began to arrive I was asked to step out of the office. I sat in the stairwell on the cold, stone steps that had been worn down by thousands of feet over the long history of the building. I waited patiently for the police to finish their preliminary investigations, fiddling with my phone in an effort to pass the time. I watched as a series of officers marched past laden with boxes packed with evidence. I called Carol and told her an abridged version of what had happened. She was audibly concerned but I reassured her that I would be home as soon as I was finished making my statement.

It was another twenty minutes before DS Burton left the crime scene and escorted me to his car. The journey to the 'A' Division headquarters in Stewart Street lasted only two minutes. The station is a stone's throw from where the M8 cuts a swathe through the north of Glasgow city centre.

I was shown into a bleak interview room and given a cup of disgusting coffee. The room was stuffy and airless, devoid of character. I sat for an hour with no sign of anyone coming to take my statement. A splinter of anxiety began to work its way into my mind. Another hour passed and the splinter had grown into a full-size log. I could feel a paralysing fear begin to take hold of me. Sweat formed on my brow as the heat of the room affected me and my imagination started to get the better of me.

When DS Burton arrived with a colleague, who was introduced as Detective Inspector McGovern, the look on their faces told me that my fears were being realised and I was no longer a witness but their chief suspect.

***

McGovern looked like Burton's comedy double act partner. He was a lot shorter than Burton at about five feet ten. He was stout, with a round face which was topped by a pathetic ten strand comb over and decorated with a moustache that resembled a shoe brush balanced on his top lip.

He was dressed in a shabby brown suit, a yellow shirt that was fraying at the collar and a grubby blue tie. He was carrying a plastic cup of coffee, which sloshed on to the floor as he walked into the room.

He put his drink down, pulled a chair from the opposite side of the table, spun it round and sat astride it with the back facing me.

"Mr Campbell, Mr Campbell. You've got quite a few questions to answer." I could see traces of food in the thick hairs of his upper lip. Below the crumbs his smile was that of a creepy uncle.

"I told your sergeant all I know." I could feel my voice begin to crack with the tension of the situation I found myself in.

"Well, you've maybe not told us everything, maybe your memory is a little wanting, it happens when you suffer a shock. So I would like you to tell me the full story, from the start."

I repeated the story that I had given to Burton. McGovern nodded in places and made a show of writing on his pad at certain points in my monologue.

He tapped a pencil on the bristles of his moustache. "Mmmm, how much did Mr Jamieson offer to pay you for your services?"

I cringed inwardly as I knew exactly what the reaction would be. "Twenty thousand pounds."

"Twenty grand?" He whistled and turned to his partner, who was standing leaning against an internal window, his face a passive mask. "We're in the wrong side of the business, Mark. Twenty grand for something that would take a couple of days at most. Looks like you and me should be working in the private sector." He said all this wearing a grimace that I think he thought was a smile. He didn't look like a man whose face got much practice at being happy.

He turned back to me. "Isn't that a lot of money for a simple task like that, Mr Campbell?"

"Yes, I suppose it is. I said that to Mr Jamieson but he insisted that he wanted me to take it to ensure my discretion." I was being honest but even to my ears it sounded like a load of crap.

"I suppose twenty grand would buy a lot of discretion, particularly if you needed an assassin." He dropped the bombshell like he was delivering a punchline.

"What?" I exclaimed. I had thought that the hacking of the computer would be the worst of my troubles but this was a much bigger concern.

"See Mr Campbell, we know how much the going rate is for having someone killed in this city. What you've been paid is more in line with that, rather than what some scumbag leech gets for gathering information, don't you think?"

"This is ridiculous. I've never even held a gun, never mind shot someone. Ask Ben, he'll tell you." I knew I sounded desperate and if I was sitting on the other side of the desk I probably wouldn't have believed me.

"Well, there's an interesting problem. Mr Jamieson is currently unavailable. Convenient, eh? Well, for him, maybe but not so much for you." He showed me his brown stained teeth as he enjoyed my discomfort.

It suddenly occurred to me that I may have been set up as a fall guy. Was the Ben Jamieson I met capable of murdering his manager and offering me up as the ideal suspect?

"If I killed him, why the hell did I bother phoning you?" I asked desperately.

"Here, Mark, what do you think of this as a theory?" He stood up and began to move around, pantomiming the story like he was reciting it to an attentive audience. "Mr Jamieson decides he wants to finish with his manager, maybe he's getting a little greedy, maybe he's the one with financial problems, who knows. Anyway, he calls Mr Campbell here, hoping that he would be desperate for some cash as he works out of a skanky office in Brig'ton. He asks him to take care of his little difficulty and to make sure that it was gone permanently. Mr Campbell finds a way to get Mr McAvoy alone, makes it much easier and less messy if there are no witnesses. He shoots McAvoy in the head, cool as you like, thinks he's Clint Eastwood. Then he walks around a bit to create some breathing space before he dumps the gun in a bin or slings it in the Clyde. When enough time has elapsed he goes back to the office, washes the FDR from his hands and jacket before he phones us to give the impression that he is just a good citizen doing his civic duty. Him being a super-clever private detective, he probably thinks us dumb plods will fall for it, that we'd say thank you Mr Campbell and scratch our arses while the case went cold."

"Sounds about right, boss," Burton chipped in his slow drawl.

"What d'you think? It makes more sense than your bullshit anyway." He smirked at me with misplaced confidence.

"If you like James Patterson, it sounds about right. You should give up your warrant card and take up the pen, you'd make a fortune writing fantasises like that. I told you exactly how it happened." It was a close call as to which was my dominant emotion, fear or anger but neither of them were helping me.

"Tell you what, we'll give you a bed for the night, while we check out who tells the better stories and you can consider what would be best for you. If you're lying you'll be having plenty more nights at the pleasure of Her Majesty. If you don't confess you'll be hearing a cell door slam and it won't open for a long time, and I mean a long time. The courts don't look kindly on people who kill for cash." McGovern slapped the table as he said 'slam' which made me jump and unnerved me despite knowing that it was a purely theatrical gesture.

"If you do confess and testify against Jamieson then your time in the pokey won't be quite so long. I'll put a good word in for you. Sergeant, take Mr Campbell to be processed. Craig Campbell, I am cautioning you and remanding you in custody on the suspicion of the murder of Kris McAvoy."

Burton pulled out a pair of handcuffs.

I was startled by the sight of the metal bracelets. "That's not necessary. I know you're only trying to do your job and I'm not going to try to run. I've done nothing wrong." I struggled to keep the surging unease breaking over me and destroying my spirit.

"Procedure," he said simply as he clamped the cuffs over my wrists and led me out of the room.

McGovern couldn't resist a last dig. "It would amaze you how many people that come through this room tell us that they've done nothing wrong, and every one of them is a lying bastard."

My phone, watch, keys, tie and shoelaces were removed by the constable in charge of processing prisoners. He asked me details of my name and address. A tag was attached to my briefcase and I was given a receipt. I hoped that Barry was right about his software, it would mean that there would be nothing on the flash drive that would increase their suspicions. When the formalities were finished, I was led upstairs to a cell on the third floor at the back of the building.

The officer removed the handcuffs and placed me into lockup.

***

The cell contained a bench and a ceiling light. That was it. A wooden bench under a window constructed of glass bricks, which was about seven feet off the ground and a fluorescent bulb that cast a sickly yellow light. The floor smelled of disinfectant, which just about masked the smell of urine, vomit and alcohol.

I had checked my watch as I handed it over, so I knew that it was about nine thirty. I sat on the bench and held my head in my hands. My first instinct was to be self-pitying, to bemoan my situation, but it began to wear off and instead I considered the possibilities.

I couldn't believe that Jamieson had killed McAvoy. If he had, it had been an amazing performance yesterday. If he hated his manager that much, he had hidden it well from me but I had been fooled before and I remembered how costly it had been then. My instincts as a detective weren't always as sharp as they might be.

If it wasn't Jamieson, who could it be?

I thought about the crime scene. McAvoy had been shot only once, right in the middle of his forehead. It would have required someone both comfortable and competent with a gun to kill a man with such clinical ease. Gun crime was rare and assassination was even rarer but this had all the signs of being a professional hit. Jamieson's lawyer had mentioned the possibility that McAvoy owed someone else money. Could it be that they had finally run out of patience with him? It looked like they could be the kind of people who dealt with problems in a decisive and very final way.

I dismissed the thoughts from my mind as there was little I could discover from a jail cell. I could only hope that Ben would turn up soon and he could help clear this up.

I began to realise that Detective Sergeant Alex Menzies would be less than happy with me. I had apologised for my rashness of the previous summer with a large bouquet and a bottle of champagne. Our friendship was back on an even keel but it was probably going to hit the rocks again and this time it might sink without trace.

I could have asked the detectives to contact her but there would be little point as there was nothing she could do for me. I doubted that a character witness would be much use when I was a suspected of murder, even if she was inclined to help.

As the night wore on the cells around me began to fill up. One of the prisoners sang sectarian songs at a considerable volume despite repeated warnings to shut up from the constables. Another vomited vigorously, which further provoked the police officers into a volley of swear words. A third jailbird shouted into the night, telling us that the Lord was coming to wreak vengeance on all mankind apart from him; he seemed to be guaranteed a place on God's starting eleven.

In the early hours of the morning the cell door creaked open and a skinny guy in his early twenties was escorted by the custody officer into my cell.

"Sorry, mate but it's Friday night, we're always double booked." The officer said sarcastically as he beamed at me before he closed the door.

My new roommate was dressed in a athletic shell suit but I doubted he had ever been near a running track at least since he left school. The white top was stained with what were probably the remnants of a kebab. He walked unsteadily towards the bench and flopped down like a puppet whose strings had been sliced with a scalpel.

"How ye doin', pal?" he slurred at me.

"Fine. You?"

"Ah'm fucked man. Oot ma face. Bashtard polis nabbed me." He seemed to be having trouble focusing on my face.

"I guessed."

"Oh, aye. Shuppose ye wid. Know whit they lifted me fur?"

"No"

"Fuckin' takin' a fuckin' pish. How the fuck can ye get lifted fur huvin' a pish?" He gestured his confusion.

"I don't know." Although I could have worked it out.

"Just cos it wis up against Frasher's windae. Ah wis fuckin' burstin' man, whit could ah dae?" He threw his arms wide to emphasise his point. I was sure the police would have been less than impressed with him relieving himself against the window of Frasers, the Glaswegian equivalent of Harrods.

"Nothing worse than getting caught short," I said supportively.

"Too fuckin' right. Ah'm Charlie, by the way." He offered me a scrawny hand which had a tattoo of a spider crudely drawn on the back of it.

"Craig." I returned and shook the spider.

"Whit ye in fur, Craig?"

I paused. "They think I shot someone in the head."

His reaction was immediate and in other circumstances would have been funny. "Fuck. Nae offence big man, nae offence." He stood up and staggered backwards to the other end of the cell with his hands raised. He slid down the wall next to the metal door and looked at me like I was Scarface.

He said nothing else but continued to watch me warily like I was going to suddenly leap over and make him my latest victim. The alcohol he had consumed began to win over his watchfulness and he was soon dreaming of a world that didn't arrest a man for 'takin' a pish'.

When the lights went out again the chorus of noise from the other cells subsided a little over time, only increasing when a new drunk, lunatic or bad guy joined the party. I would hate to work for any of the emergency services on a Friday night in my sometimes twisted city.

All night I switched between fitful dozing while lying on the bench or sitting upright feeling sorry for myself. Around nine in the morning the cell door swung open on a concerned and angry DS Menzies.

***

Charlie stirred briefly as Alex walked into the cell before his head rested on his chest again.

"He OK?" She indicated Charlie.

"Sleeping off a rough night."

"Come on," she said.

I stood up, feeling all the aches and stiffness of an uncomfortable night, combined with the strains of my predicament that had only increased my discomfort.

There was a new custody officer on duty and she slammed the door of the cell behind us and I was delighted to be on the right side of it once again.

Alex led me to another interview room. I sat in the chair and she perched on the table facing me.

"Christ, Craig, what have you got yourself involved with now?" She wasn't as angry as I had expected her to be, which I considered to be a relief.

"To be honest, I don't know. It's not what I signed up for, let's put it that way. How did you know I was here?"

"Carol phoned me. She was worried when you

70

didn't come home or ring. She asked me to see what had happened to you. You know you're putting her through the wringer?"

"I know but this is nothing to do with me. It's a misunderstanding, that's all."

"Some misunderstanding. I phoned here this morning and they told me where you were and what you were accused of."

"How bad does it look?"

"Well, it did look really bad up to about an hour ago."

I brightened. "What changed?"

"The Jamiesons' daughter came home to find her mother and father dead. Both shot in the head."

I drew in a long breath. "Shit. How's that better?"

"Their housekeeper left them at half-seven last night, by which time you were talking to my colleagues. From what I've heard, it looks like it might have been the same shooter as McAvoy. Even McGovern would find it difficult to pin that on you."

"Shit." My relief was drowned under a wave of grief and remorse for Ben and Lisa.

"McGovern's a lazy arse but in some ways I can't blame him this time. You were an easy option for him for the McAvoy murder and he hoped he could make it stick. He's not the type to investigate too thoroughly if he can avoid it. But to be fair to him, you did have the opportunity and twenty grand looks like a lot of motive. I might have lifted you myself based on that alone."

"I know. Ben insisted but I wished I had told him to keep his money, maybe he would still be alive and I wouldn't be here."

"Did you tell McGovern and his mate everything?" she asked, studying me intently as I answered.

"Yes," I lied. Protecting Barry was my only concern, I didn't want him involved in my mess.

"Right, we'll get you organised to get out of here when I've confirmed it's OK. They'll expect you to stay around so don't go planning any trips abroad."

"Don't worry, after last night, I might never leave the house again."

She left me in the interview room for about half an hour. I caught a whiff of my own odour, I smelled disgusting and every bone seemed to complain at my every movement.

When Alex came back I was processed again, warned about travelling and had all my belongings returned. I signed a receipt and followed Alex to her car.

***

Alex dropped me off at the door of our building. I declined her offer to accompany me to the flat and thanked her for her help.

Carol burst into tears as she fell into my arms when I walked into the flat. My reaction to her was dulled by exhaustion and shame. I had put her through a lot in the year and a half or so that we had been together and I had added another reason for her to hate what I did for a living.

She offered to cook me some breakfast while I went for a shower. I stripped off the now grubby suit and shirt. I stood in the shower for twenty minutes, hoping the water would flush away more than the grime and sweat, but it did nothing to lift my darkened mood. As I watched the water stream away I thought about McAvoy, my time in the cell and the murder of the Jamiesons. There was little relief in knowing that my client had not set me up as the fall guy for McAvoy's murder. He and his beautiful wife were now lying on a cold slab. Who would want to kill them? Did this have something to do with the other band members? A deranged fan? Or maybe McAvoy's past had caught up with him. It didn't matter. I decided I didn't care. I would find an appropriate time to return the money to Jamieson's daughter and put the idea of being a private detective behind me. It had already cost me too much.

I dressed in a pair of old joggers I use for painting, a scruffy T-shirt and a fading sweatshirt. When I walked into the kitchen, Carol had laid out some cereal, fruit juice and a mug of strong coffee. Bacon and eggs sizzled in a frying pan and filled the air with their enticing smell.

I ate the cereal, downed the orange juice in one gulp and savoured the coffee. Carol tried gently to get me to talk. I gave her a short resumé of the events of the previous evening but I couldn't bring myself to open up completely about what had happened or how I was feeling. Eventually she gave up and left me to finish my breakfast while she went into town for some shopping.

The food had at least recharged me physically and I felt less battered but there was no improvement in my frame of my mind. The rest of the morning I slept on the chair and the afternoon was spent looking out across the city, my head empty of anything. I had booted up my laptop to play some music. Arcade Fire seemed to match my mood so I put their 'Neon Bible' album on repeat. As I watched, rain showers passed through and I was captivated as they painted the skyline with their grey streaks which alternated with a bright cerulean blue as the clouds charged on.

Around four the buzzer for the flat entrance sounded and I answered.

"Hi, mate. It's Barry, I thought you could do with some company."

"Hi Barry, come in." I tried to keep the reluctance out of my voice, I really wasn't in the mood for company.

He arrived a short time later and joined me in the living room.

"I heard what happened on the news. Carol phoned me and asked me to look in, " he said as he sat down.

"What, does she think I can't look after myself, that I needed a babysitter?" I responded bitterly.

Barry took my sarcasm in his stride. "No, she's

worried about you. You've been through a tough couple of days and she thought that you might need a mate."

"Christ, I don't need anyone fussing over me. I just need to work it out myself, that's all."

"OK. It's not a problem but I'm going to have a coffee and if you want to talk I'll be here. If you want to talk about something else than that's fine, whatever you need."

The smell of coffee was soon permeating the flat again. He offered me a cup, which I took gratefully.

"I checked that server for you. The image seems to have been copied with no problems."

"Just delete it. There's no point at looking at it now."

"It might be important, there might be something in it that'll give you some idea why they were killed."

"Aye, well that's a problem for the police to sort out. It's got bugger all to do with me. Don't worry, I didn't say anything to them about it, so you're in the clear. Just in case that's the real reason you came round." I said it with more venom than my friend deserved.

"I wasn't worried about that, only you." His sadness at my words was obvious.

I had offended him and he motioned as if to leave. I held up my hand.

"Please, Barry, don't go, I'm sorry. I'm being an arse."

"You're right there." His face cracked into a grin and for what felt like the first time in days, I laughed.

"That's what friends are for, telling you when you're being an arse," he said.

He suggested we switch on the PlayStation and I agreed. We played a game of video tennis and like two kids in a playground, my stupidity and our brief argument was soon forgotten.

Carol arrived home about half past five with enough Chinese food for all three of us. I shared a little more of my experiences of the previous days with them as we ate , but I left out the goriest of the details.

Barry went home at nine, which left Carol and I to watch crap telly before going to bed.

CHAPTER SIX

Three weeks later I had just about put the events of those two days out of my mind. I had settled back into a pattern of insurance investigations and even refused the chance to get involved in a missing persons case that a concerned parent asked me to investigate. I had resigned myself to dismissing the exciting possibilities that being a detective brought.

I had been called in to see the police a couple of times during the previous three weeks but the ballistic information had proved that the same gun had been used in all three murders. I was in the clear, although McGovern began to float the idea of an accomplice. He warned me not to leave town. It was as if he had watched too many cop shows on television.

It was Sunday and with time on our hands I suggested to Carol that we visit the new Riverside

Museum that is a short walk from the flat.

We walked under an umbrella as the rain pattered insistently on the fabric. I was feeling more relaxed than I had for some time and it was great to be able to spend time with Carol. She had forgiven me for the anxiety I had caused her.

The Riverside Museum is the new home of Glasgow's transport collection but not all the people in the city have welcomed it. There are many who doubt the striking modern design's suitability to display the classic collection.

We arrived at the museum after just ten minutes. It was busy with parents herding children, elderly people reminiscing and tourists looking puzzled at the strange layout. It is a very different experience from the previous transport museum, with cars mounted on the wall and model ships moving past on a conveyor belt. We were enjoying our amble round when my phone rang. I didn't recognise the number on the display.

"Hello, Craig Campbell."

"Mr Campbell, hello it's Carla Jamieson, Ben's daughter."

I cringed when I heard her voice. "Oh, hi."

"I need your help, you have to help find who killed my Mum and Dad."

I signalled to Carol that I was going outside to take the call.

"Carla, I'm sorry but I can't help. The police will do

everything they can to find your parents' killer, it's nothing something I can help you with."

"Please Mr Campbell. I need your help, they've been treating me like a suspect because Mum and Dad left all the money to me. They don't seem to have much information and they've made no progress. I really need you to help me. You gave me the money that Dad gave you. I will give it all back to you if you find the killer." She was adamant in her demand. The poor girl was extremely upset and I didn't want to take advantage of her.

"Carla, it's not the money, that's irrelevant. It's just that I'm not going to be able to help you because the police have already suspected me of killing McAvoy. How's it going to look if I get involved with you? They might think that we were in on it together, I've already had the idiot detective thinking I had an accomplice." I was feeling a bit paranoid about how the police would react if I did get involved again.

She started to cry as I stood with the phone at my ear. Like most men, a woman's tears can have a profound effect on me.

"Please, Mr Campbell. I know you are a fan of Dad's music, aren't you? He told me he gave you a copy of their book. Don't you want to know what happened? Don't you want to know who killed my parents? The police just seem to have stopped looking." She was wrong about the police as they had recently used a TV broadcast in an effort to get some new information but she was obviously feeling a bit isolated and forgotten. There was no trace in her voice of the immature young girl I had first met. Despite her distress she knew exactly what she wanted and she believed I was her only hope of getting it.

"Yes, but..."

"I need to know if McAvoy was stealing from him, I need to know if that had anything to do with the murder of my parents, that's not much to ask, is it? Dad believed in you, I need you to do it for him." She was pressing for a reaction by targeting my guilt and it was working.

"Can I get back to you?"

"OK," she agreed but she seemed to be disappointed at my lack of enthusiasm. Her tone only added to the feelings of guilt I was experiencing.

I completed the call just as Carol joined me.

"Trouble?" she asked.

"It was Carla Jamieson, she wants me to have a look at her parents death," I said sheepishly.

"And you told her no, right," She stated forcefully.

"No, I said I would think about it," I mumbled.

She raised her voice, "Bloody hell, Craig. Are you really considering it, after all that's happened?"

"Look I feel a bit of responsibility to her and her Dad's memory. I don't know why precisely but I think I should try and do something. I've still got that computer image maybe there's something on it that would help."

"What are you talking about? The police have a whole host of IT experts to call on, you don't think one of them might just have found something if there was anything on that machine?"

Until now, arguments had been few and far between in our relationship but it was very obvious that Carol was mad at the thought of me being involved. Unfortunately all she did was provoke my stubborn streak and I was in no mood to back down.

"I'll have a look, if there's nothing then that's it I won't do any more but if I find something I leave the whole thing to the police."

"You won't. You'll go breenging in like some mad-cow-diseased bull in a china shop. You just can't help yourself." She stormed away in the direction of the flat leaving me standing in a Glaswegian downpour.

I knew she was only concerned for me but I felt an obligation to Ben and his family that I couldn't articulate to her. I decided that I would check out the information on the computer and see where it led.

***

I followed Carol back to the flat but she wasn't ready to talk to me. I decided to call Barry.

"Hi Barry, how are you?"

"Not bad, mate. What can I do for you?"

"Do you still have access to the image of McAvoy's computer?"

"Aye, well as far as I know. I asked the guy that owns the server to keep it available. Do you want to have a look?" he asked.

"Yes, please. Can I come round tonight?"

"About seven suit you?"

"That's fine."

I prepared a meal for both Carol and I but the conversation was very one-sided as we dined. My every sentence was greeted with a monosyllabic answer from my extremely furious girlfriend.

Around half past six I announced, "I'm going to see Barry. I might be late back."

"Fine."

Normally I would have kissed her before I left but I reckoned that might not be the best idea in the circumstances.

I suited up in a light-weight set of padded water-proof clothes for the bike. I had grown tired of my heavy leathers and these offered equal protection should I ever have another accident.

As I walked to the bike, the autumnal storm that had been brewing all day had reached its full force. The wind threw rain at me in horizontal daggers as it howled around the buildings. The detritus of the season was whipped up in little twisters and dumped on the ground with careless abandon. Autumn is the untidiest season of the year, the time for chaos to reign.

The bike was a skittish handful as I battled against the sudden strong gusts that buffeted me but I took my time and arrived at Barry's at ten to seven.

Barry had moved from the west end out to a new development that was close to Glasgow's High Street. I had been to the flat a couple of times before and found it again without any problem.

Barry buzzed me in and it wasn't long before we were both sitting at his desk, each with a cup of rich Honduran coffee for company.

My thoughts drifted to the previous time he had helped me as, his fingers a blur, he typed a series of commands into the computer. It didn't take him long to bring up the image of McAvoy's computer in a window on his desktop. He then used some further hacking software to expose both the admin password and McAvoy's own. He now had complete control of the virtual machine.

"Where do we start?" he asked when he was finished.

"Not a clue," I replied.

"What about the band's name, see what that throws up?"

"It's as good a place as any I suppose."

He began the search, looking for documents with the name and the files where the expression 'Butterfly Collectors' appeared in the text. There were hundreds of documents and it looked like it was going to be a laborious task.

We found a folder called 'Financials' with spreadsheets for each of the artists that McAvoy looked after.

"Weird that he did this himself, isn't it?" Barry observed.

"Probably habit. He started out on his own, maybe he didn't trust anyone else, or maybe these are just the official copies."

We then scanned through the e-mail and read some correspondence from a lawyer representing Jim Harris. The mails were written in a strained formal English but the message was clear. Harris was convinced that McAvoy was stealing a significant share of the band's royalties. Harris was definitely pissed at McAvoy and money was always one of the most common reasons for murder. I wondered if Harris would benefit from a greater share of the band's royalties after Ben's murder. The death of a band member usually increased interest from the public and as a result, record sales.

We gave up around midnight, having learned little that we didn't know and nothing that proved beyond doubt that McAvoy had been doing what he had been suspected of. Barry copied the relevant files on to his hard drive and then to a 16GB USB flash drive for me to take away.

I thanked him and went home through the wreckage of the storm that had almost blown itself out, weaving past fallen trees, scattered branches and a shattered billboard.

***

Carol was in bed by the time I arrived home. I wasn't feeling particularly tired and decided to have another late-night read of the Butterfly Collectors story.

Positive Force

The band's first album, Positive Force, was recorded at a small studio in an old farm near Oxford that had been used in the past by The Cure and Keane. The recording sessions began on November 3rd 1991. The first few sessions were plagued by problems as the band's nerves got the better of them. They were frequently unable to play due to uncontrollable laughing fits, an excess of alcohol or a combination of the two.

The divide that had occurred between Jim Harris and Ben Jamieson over their approach to the band began to appear. Harris was frustrated at the lack of progress, frequently railing at Jamieson for his unprofessional attitude, despite the fact that Ben was far from the worst offender.

It was four weeks before the excitement dissipated somewhat and they began to get down to some serious work. The first track to be completed was 'Gilded Rage' on December 8th after a marathon 18-hour session.

Ben's vocals proved to be the most difficult part to lay down as he was his own harshest critic. Despite the assurances of producer, Lee Thomas, who told him that they had what they needed, Ben was sure he could perform the track better after every take. By the 25th take it was obvious to everyone that the vocals Ben had recorded were not going to be improved upon. Lee Thomas persuaded Ben to sit down and listen carefully to what they had already recorded. Lee's arguments and massaging of the singer's ego convinced Ben that the 16th take was the best and that he wouldn't be able to better it.

In the wake of that discussion Ben began to trust Lee more. The choice of producer had been another contentious issue between Jim and Ben. Ben wanted a big name but Jim was convinced after hearing the albums Lee had produced for other bands, that he would be a better fit for their sound. He believed that Thomas' style - simple production that allowed every instrument to excel - was perfect for the band. This was the reason that the record company had suggested him in the first place but that alone was enough to cause Ben to rebel and argue against it. Ben thought they needed to have a more lavish production but Jim believed that a more natural sound that captured the band's live appeal made more sense. In the end only the threat of the record company's withdrawal of support had made Ben accept Lee.

When 'Gilded Rage' was completed, Ben began to tune in to Lee's guidance and judgement. The band played the next track, 'Torn Love', with the same arrangement they used in their stage set. A stripped-back version with soft drums and a subtle but strong bass let Jim's guitar and Ben's voice soar, giving the track the sound that fans would immediately recognise from their live performances. They nailed it within six takes and the belief that they were going in the right direction began to take root.

They managed to lay down at least some parts of another six tracks before they headed back to Glasgow to celebrate Christmas and New Year.

Ben attended a Hogmanay party thrown by Kris McAvoy and it was there that he was introduced to hard drugs for the first time.

When the musicians returned to the studio in the New Year, Ben seemed to have lost focus. His time-keeping became erratic and his vocal performances became inconsistent.

That was when Jim began to have his first concerns about Ben's judgement. Every member of the band had smoked pot at some point but there had been an unspoken agreement that they would avoid the hard stuff. On his return to Oxford it was obvious that Ben had changed his opinion, or someone had changed it for him.

Jim told me, "When we got back after Christmas there was something different about him and I felt he was putting everything at risk with his behaviour."

On the sixth day after the break Ben arrived at the studio an hour and a half late. His movements had the languid hesitation of a sloth and his eyes were glazed. After an hour of struggling to even read his own lyrics, Jim dragged him by the collar out into the freezing Oxford night.

"What the fuck are you playing at?" he shouted as he lifted Ben off his feet and battered him against the studio wall.

"What? What's the problem?" Ben replied. He had been completely unaware of Jim's simmering resentment.

Jim shook his bandmate. "What have you been taking?"

"Nothing, just a few beers."

"You're a fucking liar. I know what you look like drunk and this isn't it. What have you taken?"

"Done a wee line of coke, that's all," Ben confessed.

"Shit. You really are a fucking arsehole sometimes. Where did you get it?" he screamed.

"I was at a party at Kris's place at New Year. A guy I met there gave it to me. It helps me relax." Ben tried to plead his case but Jim was having none of it.

"Look, if you want this band to succeed you need to give it one hundred per cent. You can't act like some junked-up rock star before we've even released a fucking record, you tit. You better get rid of that stuff and if I see you with it I'll kick your fucking teeth down your throat."

Lee Thomas walked out of the studio to see what the problem was just as Ben was apologising and promising not to do it again.

Lee recalls, "I had never seen anyone as angry as Jim was that night. The band meant everything to him and he obviously felt that Ben was risking their *future. I'd seen band members fight before but this was on another level."*

The remaining three weeks of recording saw them complete the remaining tracks for the album as well as the extra tracks that would feature on the singles. On the final day they finished a cover version of The Jam's 'Girl On The Phone' that would be used as a 'B' side and then put the finishing touches to what would become the first single, 'Glorious Girl'.

I closed the book and went to bed, my mind troubled by the possibility of Jim Harris as a suspect. Was his passion for the band and their career enough to drive him to kill his friend?

I added Rebecca Marsh to my mental list of people worth interviewing before I drifted off to sleep.

CHAPTER SEVEN

The following morning Carol's mood had improved but not by much. Breakfast conversation was at a minimum but she did kiss me goodbye when she left for work which I took to be a good sign.

I sat with my morning caffeine fix and the newspaper. I flicked through the latest stories of gloom and doom before finding a story in the entertainment section that caught my attention.

Tribute concert for tragic singer

The remaining members of one of Glasgow's biggest rock bands will reunite to play a concert for their late singer, Ben Jamieson. Jim Harris, Mark Davidson and Kenny Strang of The Butterfly Collectors hope to be joined by some of the city's top music acts to pay tribute to the singer, his wife and the band's manager who were killed last month.

The concert is to be held at the Royal Concert Hall

and Harris is hopeful that both fellow artists and fans will be keen to pay their respects. "We think it's important that the fans get a chance to show their love for Ben and we could think of no better way than to celebrate his life than with his music," he said.

All proceeds from the concert will go to the British Heart Foundation, a charity that had close links to Mr Jamieson since his father died from a heart attack in 1996.

Among those rumoured to be booked to appear are Jon Fratelli, Bobby Gillespie of Primal Scream and Shirley Manson, lead singer with Garbage.

The remaining band members have been rehearsing at a city centre venue for the big night. Tickets will go on sale on Friday through local record stores and The Butterfly Collectors web site.

It was good news for me as I would now be able to meet the band members and find out what they knew or suspected about McAvoy and the Jamieson deaths. The concert would be a sad occasion but it did offer the fans a chance to pay their respects.

I needed to find out where they were rehearsing. I began by calling Carla Jamieson.

"Hello, Mr Campbell."

"Hi, Carla. I've decided to take the case."

"That's great, thank you. It's the first good news I've had in weeks."

"I take it you know about the concert for your Dad?"

"Yes, I heard about it. They want me to appear on the stage, but I'm not sure. I think it might be too difficult." There was little doubting the reluctance in her voice.

"By any chance do you know where the band are rehearsing?"

"I don't but I can give you the mobile number for Jim Harris. It's on Dad's phone. Give me a second." I could hear the noise of the handset being placed on a hard surface as she went in search of her father's mobile. She returned within a couple of minutes and gave me the number. I thanked her and told her I would keep her updated on any progress I made.

I added the details of the number to my phone and then dialled it.

After six rings I was invited to leave a message.

"Hi my name's Craig Campbell. I'm a detective looking in to the death of Ben Jamieson, his wife and Kris McAvoy. I was wondering if we could meet up with you and the other guys in the band for a chat. Thanks."

I didn't specify that I was a private detective but I'd worry about that when I met them.

I suited up ready for another trip on the bike and rode the lift down to the car park.

***

I was getting used to my new bike. Its handling was different from my beloved ST40s that had been destroyed during a case last year but it was still classically Ducati.

After the storm had cleared the previous night, the first frost of the winter had settled on the ground. The sun was already advancing across the line of white and erasing it like an artist unhappy with their work.

I arrived in Bridgeton with the intention of completing the latest insurance reports. The car park was busy as other people arrived to start their working day. I nodded and said good morning to the few faces I recognised.

After the customary preparation of my coffee, I plugged in my Macbook to the monitor and began some routine chores.

It was eleven o'clock before the insurance reports were complete. There were no other major insurance investigations on the horizon so I turned my thoughts to the murders.

I typed up a list of possible avenues to finding out more about what happened. The workers in McAvoy's office might know something, the band members were obviously important and Rebecca Marsh might have an insight, but looking at the list there weren't too many possibilities.

With no response from Jim Harris, I decided to speak to the staff at McAvoy's office.

I rang the number I had used to contact the office on that fateful first day.

"Good morning, McAvoy Agency, Sandra speaking.

How may I help you?"

I decided to be upfront about who I was and why I needed to speak to them. "Hi Sandra, my name is Craig Campbell. I've been hired by Ben Jamieson's daughter to look into her father's murder. I was wondering if I could come in and speak to you and your colleagues."

There was a pause before she replied, "You're the one who was here before, pretending to be a lawyer, aren't you?" I could almost feel the ice in her voice crackling its way down the line and into my ear.

"Yes, I'm sorry about the deception, but it was necessary at the time," I replied trying to sound contrite.

She still wasn't satisfied. "Aren't the police handling Mr McAvoy's murder?"

"Yes but I'm trying to help out, unofficially."

After another long pause she said, "I suppose there's no harm in it, although I don't know what an amateur is going to achieve if the professionals aren't making any progress."

I let the insult slide. "I'll come in at two if that's OK?"

"Fine. Goodbye." She hung up abruptly. I don't know what it is about me but there are times I bring out the worst in people.

***

I bought a tuna sandwich from the catering van that sat outside my office building, then made myself yet more coffee and thought about the questions I was going to ask.

Around one o'clock I was back on the bike and riding in towards the city centre. The river was covered in a thin mist, which gave the sunlight a ghostly glow. Every now and then little thick pockets would drift up on to the bank, restricting visibility and making the scene look like some eighties music video.

I parked in Waterloo Street and walked to the McAvoy offices.

The greeting I received was hardly cordial. The younger woman I had met on my previous visit wasn't at her desk. The man gave me a brief nod as I walked to Ms Brown's desk. She glanced up and gave me a look that would have wilted a battle-hardened Marine.

"Good afternoon," I said as I forced my bravest smile.

"Oh, it's you."

"Hi, do you want to talk to me first?"

"No. Speak to Henry." She gestured with her head towards the lad sitting behind her.

"OK. Thanks. Is it OK to talk here?"

"I'm taking a late lunch, so you can do what you like."

She picked up her handbag, put on her coat and walked out without another word.

"She's charming, isn't she?" I said.

"She's OK. I think she's still in shock after what's happened." Henry didn't sound very convincing in his defence of his boss.

"Hi, I'm Craig Campbell." He stood politely and shook my hand.

"Henry Daniels, pleased to meet you."

I swung a chair round from another desk and sat beside him. I took out a notebook and a pen from my rucksack.

He was in his early twenties, dressed in the scruffy chic that was expected of people in the music business. He had large dark eyes, that combined with his round cheeks, made him look almost as if puberty had passed him by. His tangle of black hair dropped across one eye and he seemed content to hide behind it.

"Henry, I've been asked to investigate the death of Mr McAvoy and the Jamiesons by their daughter, Carla. I was hoping you might be able to tell me a little about what goes on here and anything you've heard that might give me a clue as to why this might have happened."

He shrugged. "I've already told the police everything I know about that day. You were here in the afternoon, I went home, then I heard Mr McAvoy had been killed. That was it really." The clear undertone was 'please go away, I don't want to think about this'.

I nodded. "I understand that but I need to try to get things clear in my mind so I can help Carla. There could be something important that you thought was trivial."

"What about the police, should I even be talking to you?" I could understand his guarded approach but I needed him to talk.

"They aren't going to be too pleased with me but let me worry about that. How long have you worked for Mr McAvoy?"

"I started in July. I graduated with a degree in Commercial Music in June. He took me on as a low-cost option I think, but it's given me the chance to get some experience." I wasn't sure if he was being self-deprecating or if he was just being honest.

"What was he like?"

"He was very energetic. He was always on the go trying to get bookings and doing deals. He used to work well into the night, every night. He could be a bit nasty at times, he would say hurtful things if he was stressed, but generally he was all right. He offered me lots of advice about the business, which will be useful, I hope."

"Can you think of anyone who might have wanted to harm him? Someone he had an argument with in the office maybe?"

He shook his head. "The police asked me the same thing but I couldn't think of anyone. He was like everyone else, he had his bad days, but I can't think of anything he's done that might have got him killed. At least not while I've been working for him."

"I came here the first time because Ben Jamieson wanted to know if Kris was stealing money from him. He thought that there might be some cash problems with the business. Did you see any sign of there being financial problems?"

"I don't know about that, you'll need to ask Sandra. He did let someone go just before I arrived. I think I replaced them, so that was probably to reduce costs as I'm not getting paid a lot, but I can't be sure."

It was proving to be an exasperating interview.

"In the days leading up to his death, did you notice anyone around the office that looked suspicious, maybe hanging about the building or even someone who was angry with him after a visit?"

"Not in the days leading up to his death but there was this strange bloke who came in once a month. A big bruiser of a guy, looked like a boxer. He always brought a sports bag with him, stayed about two minutes and left again. He didn't look like he belonged, if you know what I mean."

"Did you get his name?"

"No but he always said hello to Nancy, as if he knew her."

"Nancy, that's the other girl that works here?"

"Yes."

"Where is she?"

"She's not been in since Mr McAvoy's murder. I don't know if she's been too upset or if she's scared.

She's spoken to Sandra, though."

"What's her second name?"

"Young." I wrote it down. The fact that she knew the strange visitor and her absence may have been a coincidence but then again it might not.

"Do you have a contact number for her?"

"You would need to ask Sandra." He became defensive again as if he didn't want to be any more involved than he already was. I met so many people who were reluctant to help, as if murder was contagious and by talking to me they might catch it.

We spent the rest of the time talking about his hopes for his career. He had originally planned to get a job as an A&R man but with the record industry shrinking, he realised that it may be difficult. Artist management was his second option and he was glad of the experience that he was getting from the McAvoy agency. We talked about the bands he liked and who he thought would do well from the crop of bands coming through.

Ms Brown arrived back at about half past two and ordered Daniel to go for a walk while she and I talked.

I now had time to take a closer look at her. Her hair was dyed blonde and was arranged in a carefully created style. Every hair was perfect and she looked like the kind of woman who would pay frequent visits to her hairstylist. She wore quite a bit of make-up but it was well applied and highlighted her best features. Her pale ochre-brown eyes were both unusual and striking. There were small lines of ageing around her mouth; when she opened it I was dazzled by her whitened teeth that shone like a lighthouse. She was dressed in immaculate business attire and dangerously high stiletto heels; it was the same look but different colours from the first time we met. She projected an image of a strong, confident woman.

"So Mr Campbell, if that's your real name, what do you want?" she bulleted the question at me.

If she was trying to rile me she was doing a very good job of it.

"World peace, a win on the lottery and a house in Malibu but short of that how about a bit less attitude and some honest answers?" I fired back.

"You're a very rude man," she replied with no hint of irony.

"Let's keep things nice and simple. You don't like me and I'm not your greatest fan but I'm trying to help a young woman understand why her parents were gunned down in cold blood. As a side issue, I'm also looking to find who killed your boss. Now you can be a stroppy cow all you like but that's not going to help me to find the killer. So are you willing to talk to me or not?"

She bristled visibly. "Why should I talk to you when you could be the murderer for all I know? Maybe the police were right all along. Maybe you want to frame me or someone else in the office."

It was my turn to sigh. "What did I say? Can we

have less of the drama queen act, please? Stop the posturing and give me some straight answers."

Her cold stare told me that she wasn't impressed by my bluntness but she nodded. "Fine. Get it over with."

"Thank you."

"What do you want to know?"

"How long have you worked here?"

"Four years," she snapped. I had the feeling that it wasn't going to be a sparkling conversation.

"What did you do before that?"

"I worked in the States, not that's any of your business.'

"OK. Did Mr McAvoy have any enemies, anybody he pissed off in the time you've worked here?"

"It's the music business, it's full of people pissing other people off, it's almost compulsory." There was a strange inflection in her voice that I couldn't quite place, possibly a hint of her time across the Atlantic.

"Is there someone specific?"

She sighed. "No one that would want to kill him and the Jamiesons, as far as I know. He could be uncompromising in business, that's for sure. He's dropped loads of acts when it looked like their star was on the wane but he's not alone in that. He was driven by success, a lot people resent that, particularly as he came up the hard way."

"Do you think that Mr McAvoy's loyalty to Ben

might have upset someone he let go?"

"It's possible, I suppose."

"Any names spring to mind?"

"There was one guy, a singer-songwriter. Gary Joyce is his name. He's a bit strange, very intense. He went ballistic when Kris told him that he was cancelling his contract. I think he was taken on initially as a favour for a friend but we couldn't get him a deal. He wasn't that original, a decent voice but nothing startling, so we had to let him go."

"What do you mean he went ballistic?"

"He smashed up some of the gold records Kris had on his wall and threw a few things. I was going to phone the police but Kris stopped me. Kris wasn't a complete bastard, he didn't want the guy to end up in jail."

"Did you tell the police this after the murders?"

"They never asked."

"I'll need his details so I can speak to him."

"Fine. You'll probably find him in Sauchiehall Street. He's back busking there most days. He's short, scruffy hair, big guitar and a mod-style parka."

I took note of the description and realised that it sounded like the guy I had seen outside the Jamieson house.

"Henry said that Kris had a visitor once a month, a bruiser was how he put it. Any idea who he is?"

"No."

I could tell that she was lying but there was little chance of getting anything more out of her in the mood she was in.

"Nothing, not even a first name?"

"It was a private thing, nothing to do with me."

"Was McAvoy a gambler?"

"Not in the sense you mean."

"In what sense was he a gambler?"

"He gambled on his own ability to identify talent that would make him money. He had a good sense for how music was changing. The Butterfly Collectors was the only band that he continued to manage for any length of time and that was only because they were the first. He hardly renewed a single contract unless he was sure the artist was still popular and would still sell records. He would gamble on the next big wave in music. He didn't always get it right but the majority of the time his gamble would pay off."

"What about drugs? There's a lot of it about in music and The Butterfly Collectors had their share of scandals."

"No." The same definite and defiant answer, but it was another lie. Maybe she thought she was protecting the reputation of her boss but I didn't find it very helpful.

"Was the business in financial trouble?"

"The whole world's in financial trouble, don't you read the papers?" She was as obtuse a person as I had ever come across.

"I think you know what I mean."

"We laid off Debbie in May and hired Henry soon after. I think that move was designed to save money because Debbie was more experienced and earned more than Henry is on now. Mr McAvoy was really pleased when The Collectors song was picked up for that film. He knew that would increase the royalties."

"But that increase wasn't passed on to the band members was it?" I pressed to see if she would respond.

She looked shame-faced but said, "I don't know anything about that."

"What about the other acts, how are they doing?"

"It's a struggle now. The only real money is in touring but you need to have a name. When the whole oldies festival thing started he signed a couple of nostalgia bands, they've done quite well. Apart from them and The Collectors, we weren't making too much from any of the other acts."

"Is there anything else you can tell me that might help me?" I asked.

"Maybe you should look at Jim Harris, he never trusted Mr McAvoy and I think he was jealous of the attention that Ben got."

"How did that manifest itself?"

"There were fights. I got the impression that Jim would have liked to have been more in the spotlight.

His ego was bruised by the attention Ben got."

"Right, I'll bear that in mind when I talk to him. Do you have Nancy Young's contact details?"

"Why do you want them?"

"I would like to speak to her, maybe she'll know a bit more about the mysterious visitor, since no one else does."

She drew me another spiteful look. She reached over to the computer, typed a few strokes as she searched for the information and then wrote the details on to a piece of paper and handed it to me. It had Nancy's details as well as the address of the singer she had mentioned. I put the information into my wallet and stood to leave.

"You should let the police deal with this, nothing good will come of you poking your nose in." The way she said it sounded almost like a threat.

"Don't worry, I can take care of myself. Thanks for your time."

I left without another word being exchanged.

I walked back to the bike, seething at Ms Brown. She had pushed every button and told me next to nothing. What I had learned inadvertently from her was that there was a drug connection to her boss.

I wondered who might have benefited from McAvoy's death as I knew he had no family. He had been linked with a number of beautiful women but from what I knew of him his only true love was money. I wondered if Ms Brown's loyalty was going to be rewarded with the business McAvoy had built.

I checked my phone before getting on the bike and realised that Jim Harris had called and left me a message.

"Hi, it's Jim Harris. You called earlier. The band will be in the rehearsal studios in Anchor Lane, opposite Queen Street Station from twelve tomorrow if you want to pop in. Cheers."

That was tomorrow afternoon organised. Hopefully I would be able to get something from them that might help.

After another frustrating day, I was glad to be on my way home.

CHAPTER EIGHT

Carol was still at work when I arrived at the flat, so I poured myself a glass of red wine and picked up the Butterfly Collectors book. I began reading at the point in their career that everything began to change.

Tears and Joy

The recording for the second album, Tears and Joy, had gone well. The studios on the island of Mauritius were expensive but the tranquillity and lack of other diversions had helped to focus everyone's thoughts.

The warm tropical setting had inspired a laid-back but happy sound for the new tracks. Lee Thomas had recruited some local musicians to add some extra percussion and a little brass but it was an evolution of the band's sound rather than anything revolutionary.

When the recording was complete, they travelled

back home to Scotland to mix the album in Perthshire. They were due to work for six weeks on completing the tracks before beginning rehearsals for the tour. The initial promotion would be in small venues around the British Isles before taking the songs to bigger venues around Europe.

Ben who was easily bored, soon tired of the technical process of mastering the recorded material and after three weeks, left the others in the studio with no details of where he was going. They were used to his sudden fits of pique but Jim had suspicions that it was more than just boredom that had provoked the sudden departure.

With five days to go in the studio the band received a call from Ben's mother. She was frantically looking for Ben as his father was in hospital after a heart attack.

Jim spent most of that day contacting some of the singer's known haunts and anyone he could think of that might have seen him. He called Ben's friends in Liverpool, New York and Paris but no one had either seen or heard from him. Jim then spoke to Kris McAvoy, who was in London finalising details of the promotional activities for the album with their record company. Kris hadn't heard from Ben since before he left the Perthshire studio. Despite Jim's best efforts he couldn't find his bandmate anywhere.

The following morning, Mrs Jamieson called to say that Davie had passed away in the night. The *band were devastated as they had all been treated like family by Ben's parents while they were growing up.*

The funeral was arranged for the following Saturday and the band continued to try to contact their recalcitrant singer. They appeared on a radio show asking him to come forward but by the day of the funeral there was still neither sight or sound of him.

All of the band members and Kris McAvoy attended the funeral with their respective partners but the hole left by Ben's absence was huge and obvious to everyone.

After the funeral, they returned to the Perthshire hills. It was a sombre group of musicians who worked with Lee Thomas to pull together the final mix of the album. The excitement of the original recording sessions had completely dissipated and everyone struggled to find the energy required to finish the record.

Ben turned up at his Glasgow flat three days after his father's funeral. He learned of Davie's death through a series of messages on his answering machine, his distraught mother's voice growing angrier and more desperate with every attempt.

He had been in Ibiza with a DJ friend, Jez Cooper. They had spent their time drinking, dancing, taking ecstasy and sleeping. He refused to take responsibility for his actions and phoned the studio to rant at Jim. His bandmate was subject to a torrent of abuse as Ben blamed him for his own failings. He accused Jim of not trying to find him, of not caring about Ben or his father. Disgusted by the insults, Jim hung up vowing never to speak to Ben again.

Ben tried to contact and then visit his mother but she refused to speak to him and after three days he disappeared again.

When he hadn't been seen for three days Kris McAvoy persuaded Jim to help him look for the singer.

After a week of searching they traced him to the island of Islay, at a holiday home he had bought for his mother and father with the proceeds from the first album. The living room was filthy, littered with empty Jim Beam bottles and the paraphernalia of the heroine he had been injecting.

They were back on the mainland the next day and took him back to Glasgow where he was booked into a rehabilitation clinic. The album release and tour was postponed with the press being told that it was due to Ben's grief and in respect of his father.

I had a vague memory of that period and the press reporting had been sympathetic. McAvoy had obviously been more than capable of spinning a story. I imagined that it would have left a significant scar on Ben's psyche with both guilt and grief tearing at him.

The joy of the chapter title came when the album

and two singles went to number one in the charts when they were finally released six months later but it was a hollow victory in the wake of all that had gone before.

Carol arrived from work, looking a little stressed. I offered to run a bath for her and the cold relationship of the past couple of days began to thaw.

I had decided to visit Carla to try to learn a bit more about her parents' death and was trying to pluck up the courage to tell Carol.

We ate a simple dinner of chicken salad before I broached the subject with her. I hoped that my girl-friend wouldn't freeze me out again but she seemed to have decided to keep her own counsel.

"I'm planning to go to see Carla Jamieson."

She looked at me with a long-suffering expression on her face.

"You are impossible, Craig Campbell. Why are you convinced that the police can't handle this?"

"It's not that, it's just I feel a responsibility. Maybe if I hadn't got involved with her father, he and his wife would still be alive."

"It's Mrs Capaldi all over again," she said it with a sadness that was tinged with pride.

Mrs Capaldi had been my neighbour at my old flat. She had died in a fall when she went to investigate someone breaking into my flat. Her death had proved to be the catalyst for my desire and conviction to solve my first private investigation.

"Not as personal maybe but similar I suppose,' I replied.

"It's not as if I can stop you, so you better do what you've got to do."

"Certainly will little lady," I said in my best cowboy accent and tipped an imaginary stetson to lighten the mood.

She smiled and kissed me gently.

I rang Carla and asked her if it was OK for me to visit her. She agreed and we arranged a time for later that evening.

***

An hour later the night was cold with a clear sky as I stepped out to mount the bike.

I rode along the Clydeside expressway, up on to the M8 and then the M77 as I headed for Newton Mearns. The motorway meant I was on the south side and pulling into Carla's street within fifteen minutes.

The fence surrounding her home was draped with the remains of the impromptu memorial that had been created by fans in the wake of her parents' death. There were bouquets of fading and brittle flowers, band memorabilia and even some football shirts. The hand-written signs had been washed out by the rain leaving only faint outlines. What was once a vibrant celebration of Ben's life and work had grown faint, a pallid reminder of everything that he and the band had meant to people.

I rang the buzzer and didn't have long to wait before the impressive gates swung open.

At the top of the drive I parked the bike and made my way to the house. Carla was waiting for me at the door.

The flirtatious teenager of a few weeks previously had been replaced by an earnest young woman with the heavy responsibilities of adulthood on her mind. She was dressed in a simple black jumper and blue jeans. Her hair was washed but untidy, she had put on some eyeliner and lipstick but the rest of her face was untouched by make-up.

"Hi, Craig, come in." She spoke with little enthusiasm.

She led me into a room on the left of the entrance hall. It was completely decorated in white. The sofas, the ornaments and even the hi-fi were all the colour of fresh snow. The only exceptions were the black curtains and a line of beautiful guitars on stands that stretched along one wall. I wondered if the decor had been influenced by the song by Cream or John Lennon's house at Tittenhurst Park.

"This was Dad's meditation room. He would come here every day."

"I didn't think he played the guitar."

"Oh, no, he didn't, but he did like to collect them." She walked down the line, introducing them to me like treasured friends. "This is a 1952 Blonde Fender Telecaster, it's the first one he bought, this one is a 1951 Gibson Super 400 Sunburst, this is a 1955 Gretsch Electromatic and this was his favourite, a 1956 Gibson Les Paul Goldtop."

"They're beautiful."

I could see that they were skilfully crafted pieces of art, even before someone brought them to life by plugging them into an amp and playing them.

"He loved them." Her voice cracked a little. She invited me to sit and I picked the sofa that faced the guitars.

She sat opposite me, her hands clasped in front of her.

"How have you been?" I asked.

"Crap, to be honest. It's really tough, the house is so big and empty. I wake up in the morning and before I open my eyes I pray that I'm still at Angela's and it's all been a horrible nightmare. But of course I'm at home and it's all too real."

"I think I must be going a bit mad, I keep thinking I see one of them on the street and it takes my breath away until I realise it's just some stranger and the reality crashes in again. Sometimes I feel angry at them for leaving me, I feel like screaming at them as if it was their fault. Crazy, isn't it?" She looked at me for some answers.

"It's all part of the grieving process I think, Carla. I'm so sorry, I don't really know what to say."

"You're not the only one. When I'm out I see people I know, desperately trying to avoid eye contact, hoping they don't have to talk to me. One even walked into an undertaker's office to avoid me. I feel like telling them there is nothing they could say that could make it any worse but I don't, I just let them drift by and let them get on with their lives."

"I know." I remembered the feelings I had when my dad had died and many of them were similar to what Carla was describing.

"How are you getting on with the investigation?" she asked.

"I've not made a huge amount of progress yet but I wanted to talk to you about what the police have said and maybe get some ideas from you."

"OK."

"Some of these questions might be quite hard for you but I need to ask them, I'm sorry."

"It's OK. I want to help in any way I can." She agreed but I could see her body tense.

"Can you tell me what happened that day?"

"I had arranged to stay with my friend Angela in Glasgow on the Friday night. We were going clubbing and Dad doesn't, - didn't like me getting a late taxi. It was about six when I left to go to Angela's, we were getting ready at her flat. We had a great night; we laughed and danced a lot. There was no message from Dad by the time I got back to her place, which should have told me something was wrong. He always liked to check I was OK but I thought nothing of it and sent him a text to say I was fine and that I would see him in the morning. I didn't drink too much because I knew I had to be up and out early. I came back here at about eight the following morning because Mum and I were flying down to London for some shopping. Saturday is Marie's day off, so I had my key for the gate and let myself in. I walked into the house but there was no sign of Mum and Dad. I shouted but there was no response. I walked upstairs and looked into their bedroom, I thought they had overslept but I could see that their bed had been made. I was still oblivious to the possibilities and although it was quite cold I thought that they had decided to have breakfast out on the decking. When I went out..."

She blinked a large tear that dropped on to her lap.

"I'm sorry to do this to you, Carla but I need to hear the details," I said softly.

She took a moment to compose herself before continuing. "They were both on the loungers. I walked up on to the deck and I saw the blood. At first nothing else seemed to register except the blood. I ran back into the house and called the police. I sat in the kitchen until they arrived, I couldn't go outside again."

"Did it look like they had tried to escape?"

"The police said that they thought Dad was shot first and that Mum had tried to get up just before she was shot, her body was slumped over the chair at an odd angle."

"I take it there are no security cameras."

"No, Dad thought that the fence and the alarm

would be enough. The worst he thought could happen was that someone would break in and steal something and apart from his guitars he wasn't that bothered. He didn't think anyone would want to hurt him."

"Did the police say how the killer got in?"

"They were convinced that it must be someone they knew, that they must have invited them in. I suppose they could have come over the fence at the back but I think the police checked that out."

"This is another difficult question but I need you to be honest with me. Was your Dad taking drugs again?"

She looked shocked. "No, absolutely not. He'd not touched anything since that fan died. He wouldn't even do some pot. He warned me that he didn't want me involved with it, told me horror stories of bad trips and friends of his who had died. He was totally paranoid about it. He even warned me in front of my friends from school, he really embarrassed me." The memory provoked a faint smile.

"What about Kris, was he involved in drugs?"

"Not as a user, no." She said with surprising sharpness.

"What do you mean?" I asked, my interest heightened.

"He was the one that introduced Dad to cocaine. At a party in his house, he gave his guests a snort for free so they'd come back for more. Dad told me that it was the first time he had tried hard drugs. He kept me away from Kris any time he visited because I don't think he trusted him."

"McAvoy was dealing?"

She nodded. "God, yes. He was into it in a big way."

"Who was supplying him?"

"I don't know but from what Dad said he could get anything you wanted."

I digested this news. I had believed that there was a drug connection to McAvoy but I had thought that he was maybe a user or a small-time dealer. Carla's revelations had cast him in a new light.

"Did your dad ever mention some guy that would visit McAvoy once a month? He looked like a bit of a hard man according to what I've heard."

She thought for a moment. "No, I don't think so."

"Did the police ask you about a drugs connection?"

"No, not a thing."

"Is there anyone else you can think might have harmed your mum and dad?"

"I can't think of anyone. There was a weirdo that hung about the gates for a while but I think he was probably harmless."

"Thanks for your help Carla, I know how difficult this has been for you. I'll leave you now and I'm sorry if I have upset you."

"It's OK. I hope you can find who killed them Craig. It might help to know that the person has been caught and is in prison. I just don't understand how anyone could be so cold as to do this to someone."

***

I said goodbye and went back to the bike. Before I rode home, I thought I would have a word with one or two of the Jamiesons' neighbours. They may have noticed something on the day of the murders, something that they hadn't thought to mention to the police. Anything was worth a try to make a breakthrough.

I parked on the road in front of the property to the left of the Jamieson house. It was a Victorian blonde sandstone villa, set in grounds that were smaller than the Jamieson's but no less impressive. The gates were manual and wide open, so I crunched my way up the gravel drive to the door. I rang a bell which I heard chime inside the house.

The house was fronted by a pair of substantial storm doors that appeared to be green but I wasn't sure due to the subdued lighting.

The darkness was illuminated by a bright light on the wall and I heard the inside door open followed by the storm door. A tall, broad man in his fifties peered down at me through a pair of glasses perched on the end of his nose.

"Yes, can I help you?" he said suspiciously.

"Hello. My name is Craig Campbell. I'm a private detective," I said as I handed him my licence for his inspection. As he studied it and gave me a fleeting glance as if he was checking that I was the man in the picture.

I continued, "I've been hired by your neighbour, Miss Jamieson, to look into her parents' death."

His stern gaze didn't flinch. "The police have already paid us a visit, we have nothing to add."

He motioned to close the door but I spoke quickly, "I understand that, but there might be a small detail that you think is irrelevant that could prove important."

He considered what I said and then changed his mind. He opened both the storm doors and the internal door to allow me access to a dark hall. The mahogany floor and staircase combined with a dark green wallpaper was hardly welcoming. Although the wallpaper looked relatively new, the design was as old as the house itself.

He indicated a door and I stepped into a well-lit living room. It was a busy room, filled with large pieces of furniture, on the walls were more prints and pictures than I could count, and ornaments of all shapes and sizes covered every available surface.

A diminutive woman sat in a large, high-backed armchair. She stood up as I entered and offered her hand.

Before she could speak her husband chimed in, "My wife, Victoria. My name's Bernstein, Dr Bernstein." It appeared that he was too important for first names. It didn't take long for me to see that he was about a ten on the pompous scale.

"Please take a seat. Victoria organise some tea for

Mr..."

"Campbell," I said again before sitting on a two-seater settee that was between the two armchairs.

"Yes, of course." She scampered away, obeying her husband before I could suggest coffee.

"As I said, Mr Campbell, I'm not sure how we can possibly be of any help. We did not have much interaction with our neighbours. The Jamiesons weren't really our kind of people."

I worked to keep my little internal demon in check and bit my tongue.

"What do you remember of the night that the Jamiesons were killed?" I asked to steer the conversation on to safer ground.

"Well, I arrived home from the hospital at around eight; I'm a paediatrician at Yorkhill, you know. I didn't notice anything out of the ordinary but I believe, through the police, that the couple were already dead by then."

"Were their gates closed?"

"Yes, I believe so."

"What about in the days leading up to the killing? Did you see anyone suspicious hanging around their house or anywhere on the street?"

"There were the usual hangers on. There were always people lounging around their gates, scruffy types mostly. I used to get the police to move them on but as they kept coming back I gave up, unless they were noisy or disruptive of course. I had to call the police after the murders, there were people all over the street, blocking access to our house."

I was overwhelmed by his obvious compassion.

Mrs Bernstein reappeared carrying a tray with a teapot, milk jug, sugar, cups and biscuits. I studied them both as she poured the tea into the delicate china cups.

She was only about five feet tall. Her brown hair was styled with an old-fashioned home perm atop a plain face with no make-up. Her clothes were equally anonymous and too old for her; muted browns with little style or character. She performed the ritual of pouring the tea quickly, like a hummingbird flitting from flower to flower. She held her head low and gave the impression that she was forever apologising for some imagined slight.

He was a barrel-chested man with slightly puffy features. His sandy-coloured hair was thinning but he wasn't yet bald. He wore a checked shirt with a heavy wool jumper and a pair of tweed trousers. He sat in the chair, his back straight and rigid, legs crossed, tartan slippers on his feet.

"I was asking your husband if he had noticed anyone suspicious, Mrs Bernstein," I said when the tea was finally poured.

She was about to answer when her husband interrupted. "She didn't see anything."

I turned to face his wife, deliberately ignoring his

rudeness.

"Mrs Bernstein, did you see anything or anyone suspicious on the day of the Jamiesons' murder?"

She looked to her husband as if seeking permission to speak. He must have indicated his agreement as she said, "Not on the day of the murder, no. Sorry."

I realised she had answered my question very precisely and I took the hint. "What about on the days leading up to it?"

Again she paused before she said, "There was this strange character that hung around their gates for about three weeks before they were killed. I thought he was a fan but I met Mrs Jamieson in the supermarket and she said that the man had been abusing them. He would shout terrible things at them when they were driving in and out of the house. They had thought about calling the police to deal with him but Mr Jamieson decided against."

"Can you describe him?"

"I don't think you want to be involved in gossip, Victoria," the doctor warned.

"Excuse me, Dr Bernstein but this might be important. Mrs Bernstein?"

"He was quite young, in his early twenties I think. Anytime I saw him he was always dressed in a long green jacket, the kind the lads on scooters wore back in the sixties. He never looked particularly clean. Sorry, that's not a very nice thing to say."

It was the same guy I had seen, the one that I

believed was Gary Joyce.

"Were the Jamiesons scared of him, do you think?"

She looked as if she didn't want to state her opinion, she probably wasn't used to expressing it.

"I'm not sure but I do think they thought he was a little mentally unstable."

"I understand. Thank you, Mrs Bernstein, you've given me some information that I can follow up on. Did you tell the police about the man?"

"No, I was a bit flustered when they arrived. It was so soon after their deaths. Nothing like this had ever happened to someone I knew before."

"We're not in the habit of associating with the kind of people who get murdered," the doctor stated.

"Sorry, I didn't realise there was a particular kind of people who get murdered," I fired back. I thought I could see the hint of a smile on Mrs Bernstein's face but it was only a flicker.

"That's not what I meant," he blustered in reply.

"Thank you both for your time, and the tea." I rose and Mrs Bernstein walked me to the front door.

"I hope you can find who did this, I really liked them," she whispered conspiratorially.

"I'll do my best," I said quietly in return.

I left the bike in front of the Bernstein house and walked about one hundred metres to the other side of the Jamieson villa.

A thick hedge and wooden gates protected the home

of the Jamiesons' other neighbours. I pushed the gate and the hinges squealed in protest. There was little light reaching the garden from the street but I could see that it was a long time since anyone had performed any kind of maintenance on it. The house was equally neglected and if it wasn't for a sliver of light shining through a crack in the curtains, I would have thought the Victorian bungalow was empty.

I knocked on a door that had only a few pieces of paint still clinging to it, the majority was bare wood. I waited for about a minute before trying again and when there was still no reply after another minute I turned to leave.

I had almost reached the gate when the door creaked open and a woman's voice called after me. "Who's there?"

I walked back towards the door. "My name's Craig Campbell. I was wondering if I could ask you some questions about the Jamiesons."

All I could see was a pale face as she peered into the gloom at me. She looked to be middle-aged but it was very difficult to be sure. She launched into a verbal volley. "I can't let you in. I can't invite a vampire in. If you invite a vampire in then they can drink your blood. I wouldn't mind if you were a werewolf, I quite like dogs but I can't take the chance. Dogs are better than cats, cats are evil. Witches' companions that's what cats are."

"Eh... I'm a private detective, I'm investigating the death of your neighbours."

"Oh, they were children of the night, no doubt. Werewolves I think because they were shot with silver bullets. You need a stake for a vampire, don't you. I know who killed them."

I doubted that she did but I asked anyway, "And who was that?"

"It was a Van Helsing, the family that is charged with destroying the children of the night. They don't differentiate between the good children of the night and the bad ones. It's their curse and their destiny."

"Well, I'll bear that in mind. Thanks for your help."

"If you come again, come at full moon. If you are a werewolf then I'll know for sure and I'll get some Pedigree Chum in for you."

"That's great, thanks." I moved quickly to the gate wearing a broad grin on my face. I doubted she would be much help and I would love to have been a fly on the wall when the police interviewed her. I dismissed the poor woman from my mind as I returned to the bike.

The ride home was time to reflect on the possibility that Ben and Lisa had been killed as part of some drug war. I just couldn't see why, if Ben was no longer involved, that he would be caught up in it. I was also a bit concerned at the lack of interest the police had shown in the drug angle. I would need to talk to Alex but I would have to find some courage first. Gary Joyce was also definitely worth having a much closer look at.

***

When I got home I still felt wide awake and felt I had to do something constructive rather than stare at the television.

I opened my laptop on the small desk we had next to the large window that looked out over the river. The view was stunning but I had to concentrate on the possibility that there would be something in McAvoy's files or e-mails that would open up another avenue of investigation.

I started with the e-mail; it was a boring task that was quickly helping me to overcome my enthusiasm and making me think about going to bed anyway. I spent half an hour reading the most mundane and trivial communications between McAvoy and his clients and their record companies and promoters.

Then I discovered a thread of mail from about two months previously. The messages were between McAvoy and Gary Joyce. They started in a civil tone but it didn't take long for the tone of the mails to degenerate.

From : Kris McAvoy
To: Gary Joyce
Dear Gary,
I'm sorry that we were unable to secure a record deal for you. As a result we have decided to free you to sign with another agency.

127

I wish you all the best for your future.

Regards

Kris McAvoy

Director

From: Gary Joyce

To Kris McAvoy

Mr McAvoy,

I can't believe you are dropping me. You've done nothing to help me. You owe me. You need to find me a deal, I deserve it. Please I'm begging you to help me.

Gary Joyce

From: Kris McAvoy

To: Gary Joyce

Gary,

Please find attached a list of other agencies you can try. I will help you with a letter of introduction if you require it.

Yours sincerely

Kris McAvoy

Director

From: Gary Joyce

To: Kris McAvoy

What use is this list to me? You're my agent, you need you to get some gigs and a record deal.

From: Kris McAvoy
To: Gary Joyce
Gary,
I'm sorry you feel that way but I can assure you that we have tried every possible avenue to get you a deal, including talking directly to American labels to see if they would be interested. Every record label is facing a tough time and is reluctant to take chances on new talent.

Another agency may have other contacts and will be in a better position to get you what you are looking for.

Yours sincerely
Kris McAvoy
Director

From: Gary Joyce
To: Kris McAvoy
McAvoy, you are a lying bastard. You know fuck all about music and are only interested in old pricks who should fuck off and give new talent a chance.

From: Kris McAvoy
To: Gary Joyce
Gary,
I have to ask you to stop contacting me in this way or I will have to consult a lawyer.

Yours sincerely
Kris McAvoy
Director

The next mail was the one that really caught my attention.

From: Gary Joyce
To: Kris McAvoy
MCAVOY YOU ARE DEAD. YOU'RE A LYING PRICK. YOU ARE DEAD. YOU EXPLOITED ME. YOU ARE DEAD. YOU AND ALL THE OLD BASTARDS THAT STOP ME FROM GETTING WHAT I DESERVE. YOU ARE DEAD. I WILL KILL YOU AND THAT BAND OF BASTARDS. YOU ARE DEAD. YOU ARE DEAD. YOU ARE DEAD.

An involuntary shiver shook me from head to toe. Here was a man who was seriously unhinged. I would have to let Alex know what I had found, I'm sure she and her colleagues would want to talk to Mr Joyce.

I went to bed, unsettled by my late-night reading.

CHAPTER NINE

The following morning I was awoken by the sound of the wind propelling rain at our bedroom window with a force that made it sound like it was gravel.

I made us both a breakfast of muesli, orange juice and Brazilian coffee. When breakfast was over, Carol got ready for work and I went for a run. I pounded along beside the river down to the 'Squiggly Bridge' along the south bank of the river and back over the Bell's Bridge before heading back to the flat, soaked to the skin and beginning to shiver with the cold.

Carol was already away to work by the time I got back. I felt energised after the run and then a bracing shower helped to blow away more of my mental cobwebs as well as some of my concerns from the previous night. I took some time in the morning to tidy up my notes and enter some of them into the computer. At eleven thirty, I was ready for the next stage of the investigation.

I rode the bike to Buchanan Galleries and parked it close to the entrance before walking down to where the band were rehearsing.

As Jim had said in the message, the studios are directly opposite Queen Street station, tucked away in a dark lane at the back of the Merchant's House building that looked out over George Square. It is so anonymous that many of the people of Glasgow wouldn't even know it is there.

The facility has a suite of modern rehearsal and recording studios with all of the equipment that a band could hope for. It's ideal for musicians as it offers a professional environment at the very heart of the city.

I was directed to the second floor when I arrived. The instruments were still being set up as I walked into the room. There were cables running from guitars and microphones to a number of amps. The bass was plugged into an Orange amp while Jim's guitar was attached to a Marshall rig. Someone I didn't recognise was working at the drum kit.

"Hi I'm Craig Campbell, I'm here to talk to the band."

A technician in his early twenties looked up. "Aye, just go through there mate."

He indicated an adjoining room where the three musicians were sitting drinking tea or coffee on a sofa.

I walked to the door just as Jim Harris opened it for me.

"Hi, I'm Craig Campbell." I shook the hand of another of my heroes.

"Craig, I'm Jim Harris, this is Mark Davidson and that's Kenny Strang." The two stood and we exchanged further handshakes.

"Dae you lot no' normally travel in pairs?" Mark asked.

"Sorry?"

"Detectives, polis, dae ye no normally come in pairs?"

"Oh no sorry. I'm not that kind of detective."

"Oh. What kind are you?" Harris asked warily.

"I'm a private detective, I was asked to look in to the deaths of the Jamiesons by their daughter, Carla."

"Look mate, I don't know if this is a good idea. We've already spoken to the police." Jim was taking the role of leader.

"I know but I'm just trying to help Carla because she doesn't think the police are making much progress."

"What can we tell you that would help?" Kenny asked, he seemed to be eager to contribute something.

"I need a bit of background about McAvoy in particular. Carla told me that he was dealing drugs. People in those circles are known to reach for a gun to solve problems from time to time. If I knew more about what he was up to, who his supplier was, it might lead me somewhere. Basically, I need something that might point me towards some answers."

Jim turned to the other two. "What do you think?"

"Awright wi' me, if it'll help," Kenny replied

"OK, it can't do any harm." Mark didn't seem to share his colleagues' enthusiasm for the task.

"Have a seat," Jim said.

Jim looked a bit different from the skinny guy with a guitar who had first appeared with The Butterfly Collectors. He had put on some weight, his reddish brown hair was now streaked with a few strands of grey. He sported a goatee beard which only made him look even older. He wore a pair of stylish designer glasses that helped to bring attention his flint grey eyes.

I started by directing my questions at him.

"You never really got on with McAvoy, did you?"

He looked at me with a penetrating gaze. "He wasn't an easy guy to like, he was always about the money. I never trusted him from the minute he arrived with that poster." His voice had a nasal tone that went with a mid-Atlantic accent. I knew he had lived in the States since 2001 and it had robbed him of some of his Scottish roots.

"Why didn't you trust him?"

"I couldn't work out how someone with no connections in the business could arrange a tour that quickly," he stated simply.

"Did you have suspicions?"

"He was a wise guy, a crook. The people he knew were dodgy characters. Guys that worked the Barrows…"

"That's Barras, dude." Mark mimicked Jim's accent.

"Fuck off, Davidson. As I was saying, it seemed as if everybody he knew outside the band were like him, a shower of chancers. They weren't the kind of people that I wanted to be associated with."

"So do you think they were behind him? Financing him, I mean?"

"I don't think they were back then no, but they had muscle and maybe used it to persuade some of the managers of the venues to book us. It was just a feeling I had as I couldn't see how else what he had achieved was possible."

I needed to know what their lead singer thought. "But Ben liked him?"

"Not as a person, no. He admired his ballsy attitude and ability to get things done because it benefited us. I don't know if he ever gave a minute's thought about the methods McAvoy had used to get those things done."

"Carla said the McAvoy introduced Ben to hard drugs, what about the rest of you? Did he ever try to get you involved?"

Mark was first to respond and it was with a degree of passion. "Aye, he tried it wi' me tae. Ah jist told 'im to fuck off. Ah've done plenty o' pot but that hard stuff jist fucks ye up."

"Ah wis the same. One night in Turin, he comes up tae me efter the show and offers me a snort. Ah jist said naw, it wisnae ma scene." Kenny didn't seem to be quite as emotional about it.

Jim just shook his head. "He never came near me. He knew what I would say. I always kept our relationship at arm's length."

"Ben got a bit more involved, didn't he?"

"More than a bit. After his dad died he went a bit mental. He had to check in to a clinic and he was in and out three or four times after that. He would be okay for a while and then the least wee thing would have him reaching for a needle or something to snort."

"Do you think McAvoy introduced Ben to heroin?"

"Without a doubt, I think it was part of his plan to bind Ben to him. He liked to use it as a lever between Ben and the rest of us."

"What was your relationship with Ben like? The biography I'm reading indicates it was quite strained."

I received another withering look. "Some of what is written in that book is exaggerated, some of it is true and some of it is just utter bullshit. Ben and I were always about the music. When he was focused on writing, recording and performing he was amazingly talented. It was also when he was happiest and when our friendship was at its strongest. I didn't like some of his choices away from the band but there was nothing I could do about it."

"What about the finances? Did you all suspected

that McAvoy was taking more than his fair share?"

"We started to get suspicious after about two years. He would send us spreadsheets with a single line saying what our earnings were but we never saw the detail. We didn't know how many records or tickets we were selling, it began to get ridiculous. We were a bit naive at the start, I suppose, but as the record sales increased and we played bigger and bigger gigs we wondered what was going on."

Mark said, "Aye, we aw started tae think it wis a bit dodgy. When yir selling big numbers and the money is rollin' in everythin' is brilliant, it's only when it's the same month efter month, despite apparently selling mair, that you begin to wonder how much he wis skimmin'." There was a genuine sense of anger from him about the band's financial dealings.

"What was the deal?"

"Officially McAvoy got 15 per cent of the net profit from everything. Whoever wrote the songs got the 85 per cent of the rights money for that song. The band's share of the profit from record sales and concert was split evenly."

I changed direction. "Were you jealous of Ben?"

He stood and I thought he was going to hit me.

"Fuck no. He was the face of the band, he had to deal with the shitty media and their inane questions. Why would anybody be jealous of that? We were different people but he was still my mate, a mate I've lost just as we were beginning to get back our connection through the music." He was visibly upset and he said it with such ferocity that I believed him instinctively.

"I'm sorry. It was just something Sandra Brown said."

"Christ, I might have known. She was McAvoy's biggest fan, probably heard a load of shit about me from him. The bitch." He started pacing in the confined space of the room.

"Sit doon man, we're aw upset and the guy's jist tryin' tae help. She's probably upset as well." Mark stood and gently eased his friend back into his chair.

I turned my attention to Mark and Kenny. "Who do you think would have done this? Is there anybody you can think of, some Chapman wannabe maybe?"

Kenny shook his head. "If we wur in the States, ah wid say aye but no o'er here. Don't get me wrong, we've hud oor fair share o' crazies. There was this bird used tae send Ben her used knickers, skid marks an' everythin'." The others joined him in laughing at the memory.

"God aye, remember that? And that guy that sent you pictures o' his boaby, remember Jim," Mark added.

Jim gave a visible shudder. I laughed with them, glad that some of the tension in the room had been released.

"But there was nothing violent?"

"There wis some bad stuff efter that boy died at the

party, remember?" Kenny said.

"I remember that. Can you tell me what happened that night?"

Jim replied, "It was the first night of the tour, a private gig for the fan club, here in Glasgow. McAvoy had organised a big bash to celebrate the launch of the album and the new tour. A young lad, in his teens if I remember correctly, was there. He had a bad reaction to some ecstasy that the police thought he had brought with him. There was nothing anyone could do for him. It was a real tragedy."

"We did get some threats then. There wis some nasty letters efter it," Kenny added.

"Did you report them to the police?"

"Aye, and ah think they spoke tae wan or two and they were warned no' tae dae it again but it aw calmed doon efter a while. When yir in this business ye attract the weirdos."

"The band split soon after."

Jim nodded sadly. "It was too much. The fights about money had been getting worse for a year or two. I felt that Ben was partly to blame for the death because of his drug problems. Of course that was a load of crap but it was just so intense at the time. We had made a brilliant album, our best work and it was all overshadowed by the death. We were devastated for the lad and his family."

"What about you two?"

"Much the same really. Tae be fair ah think Ben felt

a bit responsible himsel'. That's why he chucked the drugs completely. It wis shite though, that album was brilliant. If we'd toured efter it we would have been huge." I could see the hurt of that time on Kenny's face as he spoke. Mark nodded his agreement.

"Have any of you heard of a guy called Gary Joyce?"

They all shook their heads and said no.

"Is there anybody else I could speak to?"

Jim answered, "You could try Innes McEwan, he was our roadie and then he went to work for Ben. He might know more about what went on after the band split."

"Is that him?" I pointed to the technician in the studio.

"No, that's Paul. He's joined us for the tribute show. Contact Sandra Brown, she'll have Ian's details. The funeral was the first time I had seen him in years and we didn't talk for very long even then."

"Are you going to do the tour?" I asked as a fan.

"No. We're not complete without Ben, no one could replace him."

"I suppose not. Thanks for your help guys." I handed each of them my business card and asked them to get in touch if they could think of anything else.

***

I left the studio and walked back to the bike. I rode to Bridgeton and went in to the office to make some phone calls.

I rang McAvoy's office, Henry answered and I asked him if I could speak to Sandra Brown.

"Ms Brown, it's Craig Campbell."

"Yes." Abrupt to the point of rudeness once again. I wondered how she ever got a job as anyone's personal assistant.

"I would like to speak to Innes McEwan, one of the Butterfly Collectors' roadies."

"I know who he is."

"Do you have his contact details, please?"

"What do you want to speak to him about?"

My patience finally snapped. "Take a wild guess. Now can I please have the details?"

The phone clicked. I looked at the handset in shock. She had hung up on me. I seethed a little before realising that Carla would probably have the information I needed.

A quick call to Carla and I had McEwan's details. She warned me that he was a bit of a shambles and advised me that it might be better to turn up on his doorstep unannounced. She told me that he wasn't brilliant at keeping appointments.

I also asked her for the number for Rebecca Marsh which she was able to supply.

My final call was to Alex. I had been storing up courage and prepared myself for an onslaught but I had to let her know my concerns.

I rang her mobile. "Craig, hello?" she didn't sound

too annoyed to hear from me but then she didn't know why I was calling.

"How are you, Alex?"

"I'm good but I've got a feeling that it might change depending on what you've got to say. Is this a social call?"

"Eh... no."

"Oh God, what now?" She asked with more than a little exasperation.

"Carla Jamieson has asked me to help her." It was the truth, if not quite the whole truth.

"Please tell me it's to find her pet kitten and nothing to do with her parents' murder."

"Not exactly."

"Oh Craig, what does it take for you to stop sticking your nose where it could get shot off?" There was a hint of anger now.

"Look, I know it's not what you wanted to hear but I need to tell you what I've discovered."

She sighed. "OK. What have you discovered?"

"You said that McGovern wasn't the brightest spoon in the drawer but could he be on the take?"

"What?" she exclaimed.

"What would you say was the biggest link between the music world and the criminal world?"

"Other than anything recorded by Jedward, drugs, obviously."

"So if there are three deaths related to a single

music act you might at least expect a cop to ask about a drugs connection?"

"Yes, of course."

"So why hasn't McGovern?"

"Because he's as incompetent arse, because he's got a better lead, I don't know." I could hear the tiniest trace of doubt in her voice.

"That's one explanation, or maybe he's scared to ask the question because he knows more than he's letting on."

"Craig, this is a flight of fantasy. I know he's an idiot but I doubt that he's on the take."

"OK but here's something to think about. McAvoy was dealing drugs. The people who helped him get started in the music business were probably supplying him. Think that's a motive for murder?"

She hesitated before replying, "Yes but where do the Jamiesons fit in?"

"I'm not sure but Ben did have his share of drugs problems in the past. Surely it must be worth considering at least," I insisted.

"OK. I'll think about it. Is there anything else we've missed?" she asked sarcastically.

"Has anybody spoken to Gary Joyce? He was a client of McAvoy's for a while."

"I'm not sure, why?"

"The guy is mental. Check McAvoy's e-mails and you'll see what I mean."

"How do you know what's in his mail?" I could hear the professional in her pushing aside our friendship.

"It's better you don't ask."

"Craig, you strain our relationship to its limits, you know?" Thankfully she sounded more irritated than angry.

"I know, believe me I'm sorry."

"OK, leave it with me. I'll speak to some people and we'll have a look."

"Thanks."

"Craig, you've done well, now please leave this to me. I promise I'll make sure that the right questions are asked."

"Yes, Alex, there's just one or two more people I need to speak to."

"Craig!"

"Cheers, bye." I ended the call before she could begin another lecture.

I then rang the number that Sandra Brown had given me for the disgruntled singer, Gary Joyce. I listened to his voicemail greeting, which was bright and cheerful, not what I was expecting. I left a message but then I thought that I would look for him on his busking beat.

I had one more call to make but Rebecca Marsh, the band's biographer was also unavailable and I left another message. I was hoping she might have some insight into the relationships within and around the band. I was hoping that she knew more than she had been allowed to publish.

***

I rode back into town and parked the bike in Milton Street.

A short walk took me to Sauchiehall Street, one of the city's most famous shopping areas. It is now like many high streets across the country, populated by a number of empty shops with desperate 'To Let' and 'For Sale' signs hanging despondently outside.

I walked as far the unit, that up until recently had been a record shop, before I spotted the man in the green parka. Joyce was playing in the shelter of the shop entrance getting both protection from the elements and an acoustic boost for his music. He was playing a left-handed, blue Yamaha electric acoustic guitar. It was plugged into a small Marshall amp which helped to carry his accomplished playing to the passers-by. A small crowd had gathered to hear him play the Oasis tune 'Don't Look Back In Anger'.

I stood and listened to him play for a short time before I took out a business card, wrote on the back of it and dropped it along with some coins into his guitar case. It invited him to join me in the coffee shop in Waterstones so we could have a chat.

I crossed to the other side of the street into the bookshop and down into the basement cafe. I ordered a cappuccino and found myself a seat not far from the counter. I browsed the internet on my phone while I enjoyed the reviving drink.

My coffee was nearly finished before I saw the young musician appear with his guitar case strapped to his back, carrying his small amplifier.

He looked around the seats wondering who had left the mysterious note. I rose to meet him.

"Gary, hi I'm Craig Campbell."

"Hello." He looked nervous and shook my hand reluctantly. He then reached into his pocket, took out a small bottle of anti-bacterial wash and proceeded to clean his hands.

"What's this about?" he asked warily.

"I want to talk to you about Kris McAvoy." He immediately stiffened and I thought he was going to bolt. "I just want a chat, that's all. Take a seat. Can I get you a drink?"

The momentary indecision passed and he plumped for a bottle of water. When I returned to the table he was sitting with his guitar leaning up against his left leg, his other leg was bouncing up and down in agitation. When I offered him the water he wrapped a napkin around the bottle before taking a drink.

I noticed that the spoon I had used to stir my coffee had been wiped clean and laid on a clean napkin on the table, equidistant from two of the edges of the table.

"You play and sing well," I said as a way of starting the conversation.

"Thank you," he replied modestly. Although he was facing me, his eyes were focused somewhere over my shoulder rather than on my face. His hands were clasped in front of him, his thumbs rolled around one another as if he was using them to comfort himself. His whole body seemed to be a bundle of nervous energy.

"How long have you been playing?"

"A long time. I started when I was six."

I didn't think there was much point in continuing with small talk. "You were a client of Mr McAvoy, I believe."

"Yes." The question only heightened the stress that radiated from him in waves.

"It didn't end well, did it?"

"No."

It looked like getting a banker to hand back his bonus would be easier than extracting information from Gary Joyce. "You sent Mr McAvoy some e-mails, one of them was very threatening."

For the first time he looked me in the eye. His grey-blue eyes were dispassionate as he said, "He treated me badly. I was not well when I wrote that letter. He had put me under a lot of stress."

"Because the agency dropped you?"

"Yes. He was wrong. He didn't work hard enough to get me a deal." The undercurrent of anger that ran through him began to surface.

I thought I would try to provoke a further reaction from him, to see how deep the feelings of resentment ran. "It can't have been easy for you. It's obvious you are a talented musician, it's tough on new artists these days."

"Yes, they would rather stick with has-beens than give new people like me a chance." The facade cracked further as his voice rose.

"And you were very angry with McAvoy and The Butterfly Collectors, weren't you?"

He rolled his eyes. "Of course I was. They weren't even a band any more but McAvoy was going to tour them again." His rolling thumbs had gathered pace and were now whirring round like an out of control dynamo.

"Is that why you parked yourself outside the Jamiesons' gate for weeks on end? Is that why you killed McAvoy and the Jamiesons, because you were so angry?" I said it quietly, as if asking him what time it was.

Suddenly he became very still. "I did not kill anyone. I wouldn't do that." He said it with an incredible intensity, each word fired through tightly gritted teeth.

"Well, you threatened to kill them all in that mail you sent. You told McAvoy that 'You and all the old bastards that stop me from getting what I deserve' are dead. Didn't you?"

Tears began to form in his eyes and suddenly I felt some sympathy for him. "I have already said that I was ill when that mail was sent. I have been to see a doctor who has helped me deal with the stress, that's behind me now."

"Why did you harass the Jamiesons then?"

"I didn't harass them. I wanted him to tell Jamieson that I deserved my chance. I wanted to play for him, so he could see I had real talent, but he wouldn't give me a chance. He said that he had nothing to do with McAvoy's decisions. He was only a client."

"If that's the case you must know something about what went on. You were outside the Jamieson house for weeks. Did you see something?"

His shoulders seemed to relax but only slightly. "There were always people going in and out every day. There was a guy on a motorbike the day before they were killed."

"That was me."

"Oh. Then there was Jim Harris. He went in the afternoon they were killed and he hadn't come out again by the time I left at four o'clock."

"Are you sure it was Harris?"

"Yes, I know what all the has-beens look like. I had seen him going in a couple of times before. That day I was thinking of asking him to listen to my songs when he came out but I got bored waiting on him."

"What time did he go in?"

"About two, I think. It's time for me to go now." Before I could react he stood up, picked up his guitar case and walked away.

There was little doubt that he had problems but I couldn't quite imagine him being cool enough to shoot someone in the head. The information about Jim Harris could be significant and I decided that I would have to have another chat with the guitarist. Having reached another impasse, I hoped that Innes McEwan would have something worthwhile to tell me.

***

The address that Carla had given me for McEwan was just outside the north of the city in a village called Torrance.

On the way, I rode past the industrial estate where I had first seen Carol and where she still worked. I continued out Balmore Road and into the country-side. It was just over five miles from the city centre but it was a world away from the bustling hive of Glasgow's crowded streets.

The village lies on the approaches to the Campsie Hills, the little spur of the Trossachs that are them-selves a gentle introduction to Scotland's rugged mountain ranges.

McEwan lived in a small terrace of what was prob-ably once council stock. His house was fronted by the untidiest garden on the row. A scruffy lawn was competing with weeds and the weeds seemed to be winning. The hedge had a life of its own, branches growing in every direction, and a pathetic rose bush waved erratically in the breeze.

There was no sign of a doorbell so I knocked on the wooden door, which was covered in cracked and peeling varnish. After a minute with no reply I knocked again. I was about to walk away when I heard a key rattle in the lock. There were two more locks and apparently a couple of security chains to be released before the door finally opened. Mr McEwan was obviously very security conscious.

An emaciated man with sunken cheeks looked at me with bleary red eyes.

"Whit dae ye want?"

I took out my private investigator licence and showed it to him. "I'm Craig Campbell, I'm investigating the Butterfly Collectors murders."

"Ah cannae read that withoot ma glesses."

"I'll wait if you want to get them."

"Gie's a minute."

He shut the door and turned one of the locks. He was back within a minute. He checked my ID and invited me in.

He led me through a short hall into a spacious living room. The inside of the house was tidier than the outside, or for that matter its occupant. It wouldn't have been too difficult to achieve as there was very little to be seen in the room. A sofa, two armchairs, a television and a sideboard. There were no ornaments or pictures, nothing that made it feel like a home; I don't suppose that life on the road had given him much chance to collect things.

"D'ye want a cuppa?"

"No, I'm fine, thanks."

"Awright if ah huv wan?"

"Of course."

He walked to a small kitchen, which was attached to the living room. He spent a few minutes making the drink while muttering to himself. I studied him as he worked.

I reckoned him to be in his early fifties. Despite a mainly bald head he had manufactured a pony tail from the little rim of hair that surrounded the back of his skull. He was incredibly thin with bones obvious on his arms, hands, head and even the top of his bare feet. He was dressed in a grey stained Sex Pistols T-shirt that might once have been black, in combination with faded and patched jeans.

He came back into the living room with his coffee in one hand and an unlit cigarette in the other.

"Awright if ah smoke?" he asked.

As it was his house I didn't feel I had any right to deny him. "That's fine."

He reached down to the side of the chair and retrieved a lighter and an ashtray. I could see a can of cheap strong lager on the floor beside the ashtray. He lit the cigarette and drew a long breath of smoke deep into his lungs like it was the fragrant air of heaven.

"Whit dae ye want tae know?" he asked after he

blew the smoke into the air.

"Have the police been to visit you?"

He shrugged. "Naw. Thought they wid come but they've no' arrived yet."

"How long did you work for the band?"

"Fae the start basically. They were lookin' fur a roadie when Kris got them the first big tour, they'd been daein' it aw themsel's afore that. Stuck an advert in the NME or somethin'. Ah wis between gigs at the time, so it wis ideal fur me."

"What was your relationship with the band like, did you get on?"

"They were fine. They liked tae hear ma stories aboot workin' fur other bands, so ah wis happy tae tell them. They trusted ma judgement when it came tae riggin' up the shows. We didnae socialise or anythin' when we wurnae tourin'. It wis a good workin' relationship, nothin' mair really."

"But you stayed with Ben when the band split. Were you closer to him?"

He hesitated. "Well, ah stayed wi' Kris if ah'm being honest."

"Why Kris?"

He had another drag of the cigarette. I could see a range of conflicting emotions and thoughts were occupying him.

"Look, ah don't want any fuss, know?"

"I'm just looking for a reason that might explain

why the Jamiesons and McAvoy were killed, that's all."

"Look, ah'm gonnae tell you this but if the polis or anybody else asks me ah'll deny it. But there's nae point in keepin' it a secret noo. Ah think ah know whit goat Kris killed." He drew on the cigarette again like a diver reaching for oxygen.

"What was that?" I asked sceptically.

"Drugs."

"Why do you say that?"

He leaned forward in the seat, his cigarette sending out little rings as he gestured to emphasise every word.

"Look, Kris was in way o'er his heid with the drugs. He'd been involved for twenty years and never goat caught but ah think it was beginning tae catch up wi' him. It started wi' laundering money and before you know it he wis supplying it and then smuggling the stuff."

"Smuggling?" The shock made my voice climb an octave.

"Look, ah know you're gonnae think ah'm talkin' pish but ah swear it. Ye know how ah know? Cos ah wis the wan that helped him dae it."

"What?" I was feeling suddenly completely out of my depth, this wasn't what I was expecting to hear.

"Look, ah'm tellin' ye. Every tour, last gig afore we came back tae Britain was in Amsterdam. Kris would pick the stuff up aff some Dutch guy. Ah wid hide it in the amps, microphone stands, drums, you name it. Always made sure it got well packed at the back o' the trailer. Customs were aw o'er the buses, always suspected the band would have somethin', but they very rarely even looked at the equipment. There wis a customs guy in Harwich that wid tip us the wink if the trailers were gonnae be searched and we would haud wan back until the next boat. It was perfect."

"What did you bring in?"

"Look, it wis everythin', man, ah mean everythin'. Whitever McAvoy's bosses told him tae pick up. Eccies, junk, crack, the works."

"Who were his bosses?"

He suddenly became guarded. "Look, man they're dangerous bastards, ye don't want tae be fuckin' wi' them. No way." He shook his head and sat back in his seat.

"Please, Mr McEwan, I need to know. We need to find who killed Kris, Ben and his wife and if it's connected to the drugs trade we need to know."

There were tears in his eyes as he said, "Poor Lisa. She wis a lovely lassie."

"Can you help me?"

"Look, they find oot ah tellt ye and ah'm pan breid, man." His fear was genuine and the cigarette trembled as he spoke.

"I'm sure that there will be other ways we can prove it was them, you don't need to be involved."

He stared at me, his pupils like pinpricks at the back of his sunken eyes. Then very quietly he said, "McGavigans."

Now I could understand his fear, the McGavigans were notorious even by the standards of Glaswegian gangsters. They were alleged to be behind a number of murders across the city, all of them involving high-ranking members of other gangs. As usual, the police had proved ineffective in getting the proof they needed against the top men but it was accepted that they were the ones behind the deaths.

"How the hell did McAvoy get involved with that lot?"

"Look, goes back aw the way tae when he got interested in the Collectors. He hud been selling dodgy porn videos doon the Barras for the McGavigans. They wur jist beginning tae make a name fur themsel's back then. He went tae them and told them that he hud this band that wur gonnae be big and that he needed tae show them that he wis the best guy tae manage them. The McGavigans gave him the money tae get the posters done and then they went roon some o' the decent-sized venues and threatened the managers. Made them an offer they couldnae refuse, kind o' shit. It wis like somethin' oot the Godfather or Goodfellas. Ah know aw this cos Kris told me aboot it. Ah wis the only wan he would confide in."

It was like I'd opened an old cupboard door and all the dangerous history that was piled in had come crashing down to bury me.

"What was their role?"

"Look, they basically owned him. First they were using the band's merchandise to launder their dirty money. Nearly everybody paid cash when they wur buyin' T-shirts an' that. It wis easy for the McGavigans to put their money in and we wash it, tumble dry it and iron it fur them. I think they even supplied the T-shirts fur a while, so it wis a double earner fur them.

They also made sure they goat their cut o' any money the agency made. Anythin' they wanted fae him, he did. He started pushin' gear wi' the help o' some o' the McGavigan crew at the Collectors concerts, cos they ordered him tae dae it. Then when the band started to go abroad they came up wi' the smugglin' scheme. There wis nothin' McAvoy could dae if he wanted tae haud oan tae the business and keep his dangly bits intact, if you know whit ah mean."

"How did you get involved?"

"Look, let's jist say that when Kris contacted me there wis some unusual interview questions. Ah hud experience, ah hud worked as a rigger on a Stones tour, ah'd done a bit wi' U2 on their first big tour, but ah hud never been asked if ah wid dae anythin' the band or the manager needed before. Ah thought nothin' o' it at the time and agreed. Ah thought he meant take lassies back fur the guys an' stuff but then ah fun' oot whit he meant. It wisnae the band that ah needed to dae stuff fur, it was Kris and it wisnae whit ye would call standard roadie duties."

"Did he pay you?"

"Aye, ah goat a wee skin fur everythin' extra he asked me tae dae fur him. It wisnae much but it helped me oot. Look, ah'm no proud o' whit a did but when ye wur in wi' that lot, ye wur in fur good."

I tried to think through the reasoning behind his suspicions. "Why would they decide to kill him if he was bringing in money?"

"Look, that's just it. The money wis dryin' up fur the legit business. Maybe Kris decided he needed to get some of the drugs stuff fur himsel'. If they caught him, well ye can imagine the rest."

"What about Ben?"

"Maybe Ben knew whit wis goin' oan, maybe they're jist fuckin' mental and decided tae make an example o' Ben and Lisa. Ah don't know. It's no' as if ye're dealing wi' rational people."

"Why are you telling me all this?"

"Look, ah'm worried that ah'll be next. Somebody else needs tae know afore it's too late, know whit ah mean?"

I was so stunned that I wasn't sure what to say to him. Now I knew I was in way over my head but if McEwan was reluctant to be a witness, how would I convince Alex and her colleagues?

"Would you not be better going to the police? They

would be able to protect you."

He shook with laughter, a hearty full-blooded laugh which sounded strange coming from his thin frame. It ended in a racking cough before he said, "Look, The FBI, CIA, MI5, Special branch and Dirty fuckin' Harry aw the gither couldnae protect me fae the McGavigans, son."

"Do you think McAvoy would have tried to get out from under them by going to the police?"

"Might huv, ah suppose. But he never struck me as a grass, he wisnae that brave."

"What about you? What are you doing now?"

"Waitin' oan the next gig. Look, it's jist the life that roadies huv. Ah hate bein' in wan place aw the time but ah've no' hud work for near two year. Auld and forgotten, that's me." He looked a broken man, excluded from the only life he had ever known and loved.

"If you're so worried about the McGavigans could you not go abroad?"

"Nae money. Spent it as ah goat it, thought that ah wid be oan the road 'til they put me in a boax. Widnae matter oanyway, they wid find me unless ah wis oan the moon."

There didn't seem to be an awful lot more he could tell me, so I stood to leave. "Thanks for your help, Mr McEwan, take care."

"Innes, jist caw me Innes." He attempted a smile but somehow it seemed forced.

"Thanks Innes."

I offered my hand, he gripped it fiercely and said, "Look, son. Ah mean it, ye cannae tell a soul whit a tellt ye the day. No 'til ah'm deid, oanyway."

"OK."

"Promise me."

"I promise." He let my hand go and escorted me to the front door.

I handed him my card before I left. "If you need anything or think of something that might help, give me a bell."

I walked back down his path with my head spinning. I was stuck in a deep hole and didn't know how to dig myself out of it.

***

Carol was in the flat when I arrived back. She could tell that there was something wrong as soon as I walked into the living room.

"What's up?" she asked immediately.

"It's complicated but I can't tell you why."

'Mmm. That sounds ominous."

"I think I am truly in too deep this time. This has got more strands than a spider's web and they all radiate from one place, trouble."

"Speak to Alex, then speak to Carla and tell her you can't do any more."

"I wish it was that simple."

"She stood in front of me and studied me. "You're beginning to scare me, Craig."

"I'm sorry. I'll need to try and work it out." I was attempting to reassure her but if I was honest, I was more than a little scared myself.

We decided to order some pizza as neither of us felt like cooking.

We ate the pizza with little enthusiasm and sat watching TV. We were about to go to bed around eleven when the door buzzer sounded.

"Hello?"

"Craig Campbell, it's DCI McGovern, I need to speak to you about a murder."

"I thought we'd been through all this already, what are you doing here at this time of night?" I was tired and McGovern was the last person I wanted to see.

"No, Mr Campbell, Im talking about the murder of Innes McEwan."

CHAPTER TEN

I pressed the button to allow McGovern into the building and turned to Carol.

"It's the police, a guy I went to visit today's been murdered."

"Craig, what's this about?"

"I promise I'll tell you later but I don't trust this detective, I might have to be a bit economical with the truth, but don't worry."

"Bloody hell, you tell me the police are here about a murder and then tell me not worry. What else am I supposed to do?"

There was a knock on the flat door. I opened it to McGovern and a female detective I hadn't met previously.

"This is DC Linden," McGovern said. He flashed his warrant card as she simultaneously showed hers.

"Come in."

They walked into the living room where Carol was sitting, looking very apprehensive.

"Carol, this is Detective Inspector McGovern and Detective Constable Linden."

"Hello," she managed to say despite her obvious tension.

"Miss," McGovern replied.

Carol rose and said, "I'll go the bedroom and let you talk."

"Thanks," I said to her. My voice was meant to project a reassurance, that everything would be fine but as I didn't believe it, I didn't know why Carol would.

When she was gone McGovern said, "OK if we sit?"

"Of course, sorry."

He sat but the DC seemed to be happy to stand and took out her notebook and pen.

"We found this in Innes McEwan's house, beside his body. He was shot once between the eyes, sound familiar?"

He held up a clear plastic evidence bag with my card inside.

"Care to explain what you were doing there?"

"I went to visit him this afternoon," I struggled to say as I could feel my body shaking.

"Campbell, you're developing a bad habit of being where people turn up dead. What were you doing there?"

"I went to speak to him about the Butterfly Collectors and Kris McAvoy."

He turned to Linden. "You see Sharon, this bawbag thinks he's fuckin' Magnum P.I. He doesn't think that us daft polis can detect the smell of a fart in a fucking spacesuit." He was angry and this time there was no act to it.

His subordinate smiled politely but looked a little embarrassed. I wondered if he only had partners to play the straight man for his sparkling wit.

He directed his attention to me again. "So what have you learned, Mr Magnum? Please enlighten me with your amazing detection skills."

I bit back a retort. "Nothing. We spoke about how the band and McAvoy got together. I asked him how he started working for the band. Then we talked about who he thought might have wanted to kill Ben and McAvoy but he seemed as puzzled as you are. He was a poor soul, didn't seem to be able to remember much, but they say that's what happens when you smoke pot."

He bristled at my little dig about him not knowing who had committed the murders. "See Sharon, the private sector's not all it's cracked up to be. You know what Campbell? I think you're lying. I'm not sure why yet but I know you're a lying bastard. Where were you at about seven o'clock tonight?"

"Here with Carol."

"Anybody else verify that?"

"I paid the pizza delivery guy at about quarter to seven, he would be able to verify it."

"Still, enough time to get to Torrance for, what, about quarter past? Time of death's such an imprecise science, even these days. Maybe you should come back to your wee cell at Stewart Street for another night's rest."

I knew that he was winding me up but I refused to bite. I was tired of his school playground bully tactics.

"Fine. I'm sure your bosses will be happy that you lifted the same guy twice for two different crimes he didn't commit. My lawyers will probably get a kick out of it as well. The terrible damage it will do to my professional and personal life will be worth plenty when I lay it on thick at wrongful arrest court case." I offered my wrists as if waiting for the handcuffs.

His face flushed purple but he managed to stay calm. "Just ma wee joke, Campbell. When I find out what it is that you're hiding though, I'll at least be able to get your arse for perverting the course of justice." He seemed to savour the thought of putting me away for something.

I smiled. His bad cop routine had helped me to recover some calm.

"How did you find Innes McEwan so quickly? It looked like he lived alone."

"Not that's any of your business but a neighbour noticed his door was open. Then, like a responsible citizen, she phoned us. But you wouldn't understand that, would you? Being a responsible citizen I mean."

He was terminally ill with all the symptoms of being an arse. It wasn't his fault, he just couldn't help himself.

"McEwan was pretty security conscious, he had God knows how many locks and chains on his door. He must have known the killer," I observed thinking I was being helpful.

"Christ, I don't know how we've got by all these years without your amazing insights. Don't tell us how to do our job," he said with considerable vitriol.

"As the bodies are starting to pile up, are you going to protect the rest of the band?"

"There you go Sharon, that's what we didn't think of. Serial killer targeting the members of a band, we should probably guard the others. Us plods is so stoopid," he finished with a ridiculous voice, before adding, "Of course we're protecting them, you fuckin' smart arse."

Exhausted by the day, the news and his harassment, I said, "Is that all, has your well of insults run dry or do you want to rant on a bit longer? I would like to go to bed now."

"I decide when the interview's over. I'm sure we'll be speaking to you again before too long. Come on, Linden."

He stood up and walked out. Linden trailed behind him after firing me an apologetic look.

I was glad to lock the door behind them.

Carol appeared from the bedroom. "Everything OK?"

"For me, at least for now. Not so good if you've got connections to The Butterfly Collectors"

"Please Craig, tell me what's this about?"

I gave her the story in brief. I didn't tell her the name of the gang involved but she's a smart girl and might have worked it out herself.

"Why don't you trust the detective?" she asked when I had finished.

"From what I gather, he's never asked anyone about the drugs angle. He focused on me, then Carla and now it's a very selective serial killer. Why wouldn't he ask? Alex reckons he's just crap at his job but what if it's because he doesn't want something or somebody else exposed? What if he already knows the connections that McAvoy had because he's got the same connections?"

"Are you going to leave this now? Let Alex deal with it?"

"Yes, I promise. I've got one more person to talk to. I'm going to talk to another member of McAvoy's staff tomorrow. Once I've spoken to her, I'll talk to Alex and Carla. Whatever I've got by then I'll hand Alex the lot and that will be the end of it for me." For once I was sincere in my desire to let the police take responsibility.

***

I had a night that lacked sleep but was filled with dark thoughts. I felt powerless in the face of the possibility of a corrupt policeman and the certainty of a gangland connection.

Throughout my waking hours I considered why four people had been murdered, apparently by the same hand. Why would McGavigan want them all dead?

There was the possibility that it was revenge, that McAvoy had done something related to the band that had cost McGavigan an extremely large amount of money and now he was killing everyone associated with them.

Could it be a rogue element within the McGavigan crew or maybe one of his rivals? It seemed like a good possibility.

None of it made any sense but I couldn't see any other explanation. McGavigan and his gang would certainly have the resources to do it and they were never likely to care too much about who got hurt.

Another possibility was the fact that the band were planning to get together again, maybe some resentment that a crazed fan had been nurturing had resurfaced.

After little sleep, I was up at six. I put on my running gear and went out to exercise away some of the fear that had settled in the pit of my stomach.

The rain was cold but there was no wind as I ran back to my old haunt of Kelvingrove Park.

The city was coming to life around me as I ran.

Delivery lorries were carrying fresh milk and bread, postmen were beginning their rounds and the buses were starting their daily timetables. It all went on as if there were no such things as lunatics with guns or drug-running gangsters. It was almost reassuring and helped to keep my thoughts in perspective.

On the way back I noticed a man putting a newspaper banner outside a newsagents. In large bold print it said 'BUTTERFLY KILLER STRIKES AGAIN'. I stopped and bought a paper.

The writer seemed to be convinced by McGovern's story of a crazed serial killer targeting people associated with the band. There was an appeal for witnesses to any of the killings to come forward to help the police with their inquiries. The lack of progress on the original murders was highlighted and the editorial demanded some more action from the police.

By the time I got back to the flat Carol was dressed and ready to head to work. She kissed me and practically squeezed the breath out of me. "Take care," she ordered.

"Will do. See you later."

I had a cold shower to further stimulate me and followed that with the strongest coffee we had in the cupboard.

As I dressed in a plain white T-shirt and black jeans I began to wonder if I should carry something to protect myself. I had no reason to think that the McGavigans knew anything about me but something niggled at the back of my mind that I would better taking precautions. I would never think of carrying a gun and the thought of wielding a knife appalled me. I had my tae-kwon-do skills to fall back on but that was about it. I was desperate to leave this case and maybe the life of a private detective well behind me.

***

I had a few hours to spare and with nothing else to fill the time, I decided to read some more of the book.

Western stars

The first album had made little impact on the audiences in the US. Grunge was still the big thing for American rock fans and the optimism of The Butterfly Collectors' songs was not what American fans were looking for at that time.

After the release of the 'Tears and Joy' album, it looked like there was a change in the American music scene and that maybe they were ready for the band as the cult of grunge began to wane after the suicide of its reluctant leader, Kurt Cobain.

The first gig on the American leg of the tour was in Pittsburgh. The venue was a 1500-capacity hall but no one in the band expected a full house. They were pleasantly surprised when a crowd of just under one thousand fans turned up. The audience responded well to the set. The new songs went down particularly well and all four members were feeling very upbeat about their chances.

"That gig in Pittsburgh was the first time we had

a really positive reaction in America. Every British band wants to be big in the States but that was the first time we believed we could do it," Jim Harris told a reporter from a British newspaper later in the tour.

They played successful gigs in twenty-two cities across the US and Canada. A lot of the time they were supporting local favourites but the stand-alone gigs were well attended too. Their reputation and album sales were boosted by the appearances and they were all thrilled to be playing the final gig in New York. They were booked to play CBGB, or CB's as it is known by the fans. It was the home of the 'new wave' bands that came from the Big Apple in the late seventies. Bands like Blondie and Talking Heads had both played there and the Scots were excited at the prospect of appearing on the same stage as some of their heroes. A large contingent of influential American music journalists was in the audience, including a representative of the most important magazine of them all, Rolling Stone.

Despite having performed well throughout the tour, on the night of the CB's gig Ben was extremely nervous. He tried to calm the nerves by taking a few shots of Jim Beam that soon became a full bottle. His lack of self-discipline was to prove costly.

He arrived at the club drunk to the point on incapable and certainly in no condition to perform. Kris McAvoy and the other band members plied him with water and coffee in an effort to sober him up but it had little effect. They postponed the start of the show by thirty minutes in the hope that they would be able to get him ready to go on and at least give the audience some kind of show.

The band eventually took the stage to an already restless and hostile New York audience, one hour late.

Ben's performance was muted and he struggled to remember the words to some of the songs. The crowd grew increasingly edgy and one young man close to the front of the stage began to heckle Ben in the break between songs.

Things turned ugly just after they had finished 'Call of the Wild', about halfway through the set. The heckler, Marty Baldini, had also had been drinking and shouted from the floor, "Hey, buddy, It's no wonder your pa died if he had to listen to this crap."

Ben snapped. Before anyone could react he launched himself from the stage and landed on Baldini and his girlfriend, breaking her collar-bone in the process. Innes McEwan immediately ran from the wings and jumped in to protect the singer. Ben proceeded to beat Baldini senseless despite McEwan's efforts to stop him. A team of security guards pulled them both away from Baldini, giving both the Scots some rough treatment of their own.

Baldini suffered a broken jaw and lost three teeth. The concert was halted as the security guards struggled to regain order among a now vengeful crowd.

The police arrived and arrested both Ben and Innes. They spent a night in the cells at the 9th Precinct Station on East 5th Street. They would have been charged had the band not been due to depart for the UK the following day. As it was, they were told that they would not be welcome in the United States and officially deported.

The other members of the band were furious, they knew that Ben had blown any chance they might have had to break America. Mark Davidson was so furious he had to be restrained when the band assembled for the flight home. Jim Harris decided to quit but the other two managed to persuade him to at least finish the European and British dates of the tour.

Jim's relationship with Ben reached an all-time low. They only spoke at the gigs and they had no contact at any other time. Mark was equally distant and Kenny only spoke to Ben occasionally as the others realised how much Ben's drinking and temper had cost them.

The rest of the gigs on the tour lacked the vibrancy that had characterised their career together up to that point. The gig in Leicester was lambasted in the pages of Q magazine as the writer felt the band were going through the motions.

As was tradition, the last gig was a homecoming affair in Glasgow, this time at the famous Barrowlands Ballroom, directly above the market where McAvoy had run from the police. It is rated by many to be one of the premier venues for music gigs in the world, thanks to the fantastic acoustics, pulsating atmosphere and passionate, enthusiastic crowd.

It was another big night for the band as this was the first time they had played the venue since a five-band promotional gig in the winter of 1990. The Glasgow crowd has a reputation for either loving a band or hating them, there is nothing in between. As Glaswegians, The Butterfly Collectors would get some leeway, but a repeat of the New York debacle or even a gig where they were thought to be coasting would probably have finished them in their home town and brought their career to a shuddering halt.

All the band members took the opportunity to go home and friends of Kris McAvoy were delegated the task of baby-sitting Ben to ensure that there would be no Jim Beam or any other substance that might affect the singer's performance.

At seven that night the band began to assemble in the creaking old hall. There was no alcohol backstage, not even the usual selection of beer; everyone was all too aware of what a bad gig would do to their long-term prospects. Ben was the last to arrive, in the hour before the gig he was introverted but just before they were due to go on he held up his hands.

"Guys, look, I'm really sorry for what happened in New York. I know I blew our big chance but we've

still got the rest of the world, so let's prove who the best band in the world is, starting right here in Glasgow."

His confidence and enthusiasm eroded some of the barriers that existed between him and his band mates. Suddenly they were a band once more. It was like they were just four guys starting out on their journey again.

There was a strangely muted reaction from the crowd as the band walked on. The story of the New York concert had been big news in Scotland and the Q review had further diminished their reputation. The Barrowlands crowd were unsure what kind of performance they were going to get.

From the powerful first chord of 'Desire Time' it was obvious that it was going to be a night to remember. Ben had the crowd in the palm of his hand and the sweat was soon dripping down from the old decorative stars on the ceiling, running down the pillars at the edge of the dance floor. The crowd were saturated as they danced and bounced in a way that only a Glasgow crowd could.

At the end of the second encore, a cover version of 'Got To Get You Into My Life', they had claimed a place on the Barrowland roll of honour. It was another turning point in their unpredictable career.

I remembered going to their second storming night at the Barrowland the following year. It was one of the musical highlights of my life.

I had been convinced by Jim's defence of his relationship with Ben but there was no doubt that Ben had blown a huge opportunity for the band. The fact that Jim now lived in the States probably reflected how important the country was to him. He was also among the last to have seen Ben alive; I wondered why he hadn't mentioned that when I spoke to him.

It chilled me slightly to think of 'friends of McAvoy' baby-sitting anyone. If they were McGavigan's thugs then baseball bats or knuckle-dusters would have been their idea of tender care.

It was time to get ready for my visit to Nancy Young, my final involvement in the case.

CHAPTER ELEVEN

Nancy Young lived in Milngavie, a prosperous suburb to the north of the city. It took me half an hour to ride to the district and then to find her nineteen-thirties semi-detached house in a tree-lined street. The trees were covered in their autumnal cloaks and were casually casting them off on to the cars and street below in a brown flurry.

I rolled the bike into her drive where a brand new black Alfa Romeo sat glinting in the sun. There were a couple of steps up to her compact and neat garden. I rang the doorbell, which rang in the hall with the chimes of Big Ben.

Instead of the young woman I was expecting, the door was opened by an ugly man in his early twenties with shoulders the breadth of a park bench. He didn't say anything as he stood occupying the doorway almost as well as the door had.

"Sorry, I'm looking for Ms Young."

"She's in there." He stood aside and pointed to a door in the hall.

The room was decorated in a way that wasn't too sympathetic to the character of the building. A light laminate - possibly maple - covered the floor. The walls were decorated with a cream-coloured paint and chrome light fittings which were all incongruous in the fine old house.

The girl I remembered from my first visit to McAvoy's office was sitting on a cream leather sofa. To her right a bottle of white wine sat opened beside a half-full glass on the surface of an ugly chrome table with a tiled top. The whole place screamed a tasteless disregard for the building's history. It was topped off by the picture on the wall, a waterfall, backlit to provide an animated display of the falling water. The kind of 'art' they gave away as a prize at seaside bingo as so few people would buy it.

Nancy was in her early twenties. She may have been attractive but it was hard to tell under the thick coat of make-up, false eyelashes and blonde hair extensions. She was dressed in a bracken brown jumper and skinny blue jeans. She wore a pair of four-inch high heels that seemed a strange choice for someone inside their own home.

"Hi, I'm Craig Campbell," I said as I approached the sofa.

She didn't stand up to shake my hand but did offer

me what felt like a damp empty sock in the shape of her hand.

"I remember you from the office. I'm Nancy."

Bench man had parked himself at the door, staring down at me from his darkly bearded, impassive face.

"Ms Young, I would like to ask you some questions about your job at Kris McAvoy's Agency and maybe get some information about what happened to Mr McAvoy."

She lifted the bottle and added to the wine already in the glass.

"What would you like to know, Craig Campbell?" she said with what I presumed was meant to be a flirtatious expression.

Despite the early hour she was already a little drunk; the process of speaking and simultaneously filling her glass seemed to be taxing her.

"How long have you worked at the agency?"

She made a show of thinking. "Three years, something like that."

"What was your job?"

"Filing, clerical, the usual boring stuff." The alcohol seemed to be making it difficult for her to focus on me.

"Did you have anything to do with the financial aspect of the business?"

"Ha, me dealing with money, you must be joking. I can't count to save myself." The glass swayed in her hand and she spilled a little of the wine on the settee. She mopped it up with a tissue, retrieved from another table to the right of where she was sitting. She put the glass on the table and started to pour yet more from the bottle to replace what she had lost.

"Tell me about Kris McAvoy."

"He was OK I suppose. I've worked for worse."

"What was the first thing that came into your head when you heard he had been killed?"

"Just shock really. Like everybody else, I suppose."

"You didn't think of anyone that might have been involved or maybe a reason for it?"

"Well, I suppose I thought about you as you'd been in earlier that day." It wasn't the answer I was hoping for but probably what I deserved.

"Henry said that Mr McAvoy had a regular visitor, he described the man as a bruiser. He thought you might have known him. Any ideas?"

There was an unmistakeable flash of fear on her face as she looked to the door. She tried to cover it up but I thought that she knew exactly who the visitor had been because he was standing behind me.

"No, he's mistaken. I was just being friendly. I'm just a friendly kind of person." The lie was plain to see but I let it go .

I decided to divert her attention. "You must have been very close to Mr McAvoy. You seem to have taken his death very hard."

She reached for the wine and took a large gulp before replying, "What do you mean?"

"Well, you haven't been back to work since the shooting."

Once again she looked over my shoulder at her guardian angel.

"I just got scared, that's all. It's scary to think of something like that happening where you work," she said feebly.

"Are you sure the shooting is what is scaring you?" I asked, to see how she would react.

I got a response but it wasn't very helpful. She gave me an angry look that seemed to indicate that she needed me to shut up.

"If the agency survives are you going to go back?

"I don't think so."

"It'll be hard to keep this lovely house then."

"No, I'll be fine I own the house. It was a gift from my uncle," she said with a good deal of pride.

"Wow, that's amazing. That's a very generous uncle you have," I said pleasantly.

She smiled and gave weak laugh with another glance behind me.

"Can he not sit, has he got piles or something?" I asked in a stage whisper as I pointed behind me.

Despite her fear she responded with a tipsy giggle.

"Who is he?" I added in the same tone.

"Eh, he's my cousin."

"Was it his dad who gave you the house?"

She nodded, put a finger to her lips. "Shhh."

"Right you, that's enough. I think it's time you were leaving." The cousin rumbled out the command, directed forcefully at me.

"I'm not finished talking to Nancy," I protested.

"Aye, you are."

He stepped towards me. I stood up with my arms wide in a placating gesture. "Fine. Whatever you say. I'll maybe pop back another time, Nancy, when your cousin's getting his hair done."

She tried to stifle another giggle as the alcohol in her system made everything seem funny.

I walked towards her 'cousin'. "Give your boss a message from me, would you?"

"I don't know what you're talking about," he growled.

"I think that you or someone very like you was McAvoy's monthly visitor. I think your boss, or maybe its your dad, was using McAvoy to help promote and distribute his drugs business. I think that poor Nancy here was placed into the agency to keep an eye on McAvoy, just in case he got any ideas of breaking your hold on him. You wouldn't have wanted him to talk to the police, for example, that would have been very awkward. Poor Nancy is now shit-scared because she thinks you or one of your goons decided that McAvoy had been a naughty boy. In your world, naughty gets you a bullet. Nancy might be family but I don't think she's really part of the family business. I know what McAvoy was involved in and I'm sure the police will be really interested in hearing all about it."

He continued to stare at me like I was a bug he was about to squash.

"Bollocks," he said before grabbing me and walking me to the door. He slammed it shut without another word.

Adrenaline pounding in my ears, I walked away from the house. It was only when I was sitting on the bike again that the realisation of what I had just done came crashing down on me and sent my limbs into a shivering fit. There were times when I felt that there was someone else controlling my actions, a devilish figure who liked to drop me into trouble.

***

On the ride to the office the only thing I could think was, what the hell had I done? Winding up the muscle of a major crime syndicate was not something that would lead to a long life.

When I reached the office, I made a very strong coffee to help steady my nerves.

As I drank it, my mobile rang and the display told me it was Rebecca Marsh, the Collectors' biographer. Relieved to have something to do I pulled my notepad and pen from the desk.

"Hi, Craig Campbell speaking."

"Hello Mr Campbell, it's Rebecca Marsh. I believe

you wanted to speak to me." Her well-modulated English tones were clipped and precise.

"Hello, I was hoping you might be able to give me some background information about The Butterfly Collectors."

"Are you a journalist?" she asked, wary of betraying anything to a competitor.

"No. I'm a private detective and Carla Jamieson has asked me to have a look at the circumstances of her parents' death."

"Oh, I see. I thought the police would be dealing with that. I had a female officer call me after the original deaths."

"I think Carla feels that they aren't making much progress. I'm trying to get things moving," I explained.

"The latest death must have increased the pressure on them to get a result, surely," she asserted.

"Yes, I imagine it would, but let's just say the lead detective hasn't dazzled me with his insights. He seems to think there is some crazy serial killer out to wipe out the band but I think that there must be more to it than that. I've discovered that there was a strong drug connection with McAvoy. Did you come across anything while you were researching the band that might help?"

She hesitated. "Yes... there were some rumours but the publishers were wary of putting any of them into the book. I only had some second-hand stories, nothing that would have stood up in court. McAvoy and the roadie were tight-lipped although Ben was quite open about his own problems."

"Did he say who had introduced the drugs to him?"

"Yes, he told me but asked me to keep it out of the book. He had a strange loyalty to McAvoy; it was almost like he thought that McAvoy was the reason for their success, rather than their own talent. At the same time he didn't seem to like his manager as a person, it was an unusual relationship."

Her thoughts mirrored my own after my conversation with Ben at the start of the case. It was a loyalty that might even have led to the murders and that was the real tragedy.

"When you first heard about the deaths did you have any thoughts on who might have been responsible for them?"

There was a longer pause before she said, "I thought the drug angle was a distinct possibility, I must admit. I hadn't spoken to Ben since the book was published so I didn't know whether he was involved in that scene again but McAvoy was definitely scared of those connections. Another reason we didn't put the details into the book was that we were worried at what the consequences might have been for me or the band."

"So you know who was pulling the strings?"

"Yes. They're not the kind of people you want to write about without a lot of evidence and the assurance of police protection."

"Did you think of going to the police?"

"No. There was no point, not without any proof."

My own rash actions of earlier looked even more stupid in light of what she was saying.

"The guys told me that there was some hate mail in the aftermath of the death of that young fan. Did you get access to any of that?"

"There was some crazy stuff. People telling them that they would rot in hell, some were long rants with more swear words than anything else but there were a couple that were disturbing. One claimed that they would all hang for what they had done and that the writer would be the executioner. It wasn't well written, the spelling was poor, it looked as if it had been penned by someone with little or no education. The other was just the opposite. It was also hand-written and it was a very dispassionate account of how they were going to be murdered when they least expected it. That the writer would plan their revenge carefully and execute it when they thought they were safe. To be honest it affected me more than any of the others I read, it was almost devoid of emotion. The other strange thing about it was that it mentioned McAvoy by name. It said he would be the first."

That certainly sounded like someone who could commit the murders in a cold-blooded way. It was disturbing.

"Was it given to the police at the time?"

"I think they all were but it's not easy to trace these

things, particularly with the volume of mail that the band received all the time. Kris McAvoy hired some security for a while but in the end, I think everyone dismissed it as another nutter."

"You didn't publish anything about it?"

"No. I covered the letters in a generic way in the book but I didn't want to give the writers any publicity. The press would have snapped it up in a minute."

"I don't suppose you know where that letter is, by any chance?"

"No, I'm afraid not. I think they were destroyed after I was finished with them but I'll check to see in case there's a copy in my files. The police might still have a record of it somewhere, I think."

It wasn't ideal but if there was a chance of getting hold of it there might be something in it.

"Thanks for your help, Rebecca."

"You're welcome. If there's anything else just give me a ring."

"Cheers. Bye." We finished the call and I looked at the scribble I had made on my pad.

She had confirmed what I though about the drugs connection. It was too strong to ignore but the letter added yet another layer.

***

The rest of the day was taken up in writing a summary of everything I had discovered and then mailing it to Alex. I felt I had taken the case as far as I could and would leave it up my friend and her colleagues to resolve. I called the Jamieson house to tell Carla my decision but there was no reply. I would try again when I got home.

I packed up and switched off all my electrical equipment, grabbed my bike helmet and my bag, and then locked the office.

The day had taken a lot out of me and I was looking forward to getting home and putting the whole mess behind me.

It was already nearly dark by the time I stepped out into the office car park.

"Hey, Craig."

I turned towards the voice but before I had completed the movement I felt a crack on my head. A white rabbit appeared and invited me to join him in a dark hole, I plunged in eagerly, chasing the imaginary mammal into the blackness.

CHAPTER TWELVE

I awoke with the smell of ammonia tearing at my nostrils. The left side of my head felt like someone was trying to drill out of it. It pounded to the sound of the imaginary miner and it felt as if the area was burning.

From my position I could see some light but the room generally seemed to be cloaked in darkness. I blinked in an effort to make my eyes focus but they were slow to react.

"Are you with us, Mr Campbell?" A voice seemed to come from the end of a long tunnel. My eyes peered down the tunnel and all of a sudden the image at the end appeared to rush towards me.

I was sitting in a chair and in front of me was what looked like a card table, the green baize lit by over-head lights. On the far side of the table I could see a figure who leaned forward into the cone of the light.

My stomach flipped like a gymnast on speed as I

recognised the face of the boss of the McGavigan crime family. Malcolm McGavigan's broad frame filled the chair he occupied like some mediaeval monarch. What was left of his hair was shaved close to his bulldog-shaped head. His jowls lifted and wobbled gently as he smiled. I knew he was in his late forties but he looked older. He was a second-generation gangster, having taken over the role of the head of the family after his father had died of a heart attack, like he was Michael Corleone and his father was Vito.

"Nice of you to join us, Mr Campbell." His voice had the throaty, gravelly texture of a heavy smoker. A glance at his nicotine-stained right hand was enough to confirm that theory. It was also the sound of a man who was completely confident in the control he had over me and the situation I was in.

"It's a pleasure, at least it would have been if my head didn't feel like it had been hit with an iron bar," I slurred a weak response.

"I'm sorry about that, my lads were a little exuberant in how they followed my instructions. Sometimes there is not much you can do to reel in the enthusiasm of the young. In case you were wondering, the smell that revived you was a little dose of smelling salts, nothing harmful." His smile became a grin that showed off a set of dazzling white teeth too perfect to be real. It was a grin with more than a hint of menace.

As I became aware of my surroundings I was

relieved to realise that I wasn't tied to the chair. I peered beyond the circle of light and could see a figure in the shadows directly behind McGavigan. There was another presence to my right; I presumed it was whoever had administered the salts. I may not have been bound but I didn't think I would be able to walk out the room without McGavigan's permission. Maybe I wasn't going to walk out at all but there was nothing I could do about it either way.

My reasoning was a little fuzzy but I did manage to ask, "Why am I here?"

"Now, Craig - can I call you Craig?" he asked, like the genial host of an honoured guest.

"Aye, if you like. What do I call you, Don or just sir?" I answered with more spirit than was sensible. It was that demon again.

McGavigan laughed and his jowls vibrated even more. "I like you, Craig. You've got some pair of baws on you. No, Malcolm will be fine. As I was saying, you're here for a friendly chat, an exchange of ideas between two people, that's all."

"I don't remember too many invitations to a friendly chat coming with a cracked skull. Is it some new part of social etiquette that I missed?"

His tone took on an edge as he replied, "I've already apologised for that."

"What would you like to chat about, Malcolm?" I thought I might as well play along, I didn't have anything else too pressing to do.

"Do you like poker, Craig?"

I began to wonder if I had indeed followed a white rabbit down that dark hole and he had slipped me one of his wondrous potions.

"Sorry?"

"Poker, do you enjoy a game of poker?"

"I've not played too often, to be honest, but I did enjoy it when I did."

"So you know the rules?"

"Yeah, the basics anyway of Texas Hold 'Em and five card stud."

"I love the game myself. First played it in Vegas about ten years ago now. I find it helps me to relax, helps me cope with the stresses of business."

"I can imagine. But I would have thought doing business with you would be more stressful for the other party."

He laughed again. I felt like a mouse being toyed with in the claws of the Cheshire cat.

"I like to play while I'm having a friendly chat. It's a good thing for friends to do, don't you think?"

I gave a guarded "yes" as a reply. At that point I would have agreed with almost anything if it meant I could get out of there and be on my way home. At least that's what I hoped would happen if I co-operated.

"Very good. A wee friendly game of Hold 'Em to help our chat along. Don't worry, we'll play for chips, a friendly game with no money at stake."

"I'm glad of that. I thought that maybe this was going to cost me an arm and a leg, literally."

He laughed again as he flicked a hand in a gesture that prompted a response from one of the figures in the shadows, who stepped forward and took up a place at the table. McGavigan made a show of opening a deck of cards and removing the cellophane from them, like a magician about to begin some sleight of hand. He passed the cards to my near-silent friend from Nancy's house.

"I believe you've met my son, Alan," McGavigan said.

"I've had that pleasure." My sarcasm went unremarked.

The cards looked tiny in the shovel-like mitts that were posing as McGavigan junior's hands. He shuffled the deck with the skill of a man who was used to handling playing cards.

The game began and, although McGavigan had expressed a desire to chat, the first few hands were played in silence other than the bets we made. I played as well as I could with my throbbing head as a distraction but he slowly ate into my pile of casino chips. McGavigan was so still it was like playing against a waxwork dummy. A better poker player may have been able to read him but I was getting nothing from his almost non-existent reactions.

I reckoned we had been playing for about half an

hour, my chips had dwindled to about half of their original amount. I was feeling ill as my temperature soared and the pit of my stomach roiled and gurgled like a slow river. Two cards were dealt on each side of the table and I glanced at mine by lifting their corners. The nine and jack of hearts. Not a great hand but I decided to see what the flop brought so I tossed a chip in that was worth twenty-five imaginary pounds. McGavigan also bought in and we waited for the flop.

The flop comprises three cards and for this hand, they were the ace of clubs, the ace of diamonds and the jack of hearts. This gave me an outside chance of a flush but if McGavigan was sitting with a single ace he would be in a very strong position. I decided that as this was supposedly a friendly game I would risk it. If he won maybe he would finally tell me what this was all about.

McGavigan made a small raise, which I matched.

The next card is called the turn and it was the ten of hearts, the perfect card for my hand. A seven or a queen of hearts would give me a straight flush. I kept my body as still as I could, trying not to betray the strength of my hand.

The increased raise from McGavigan showed me that he was confident but there was no way for me to tell whether he was bluffing or not. I matched and raised his bet. He looked over the table with a penetrating gaze as if he was hoping to see through the back of the two cards that lay on the baize in front of me. He called my raised bet and we were down to the last turn of the card, which in Hold 'Em is called the river.

I could hardly believe my luck as the queen of hearts floated down on to the table. With three hearts on the board, McGavigan could also be sitting with a flush, but I knew my straight flush would beat anything he had, even it was another two aces.

The bets mounted quickly and I had no option but to go all in by the end of the exchange. He could have matched my bet easily but for the first time he grinned as he pushed all of his chips into the middle to join mine.

"I think you're bluffing, Craig. So let's see what you've got."

He turned over the remaining two aces.

I was enjoying the small bit of power I had over him. I decided to be dramatic and turned the first card over. A momentary doubt flickered but then he smiled again as he reached across to turn over my final card.

I watched him closely as he realised what had happened. Anger shot across his face like a small tremor but then he seemed to realise that there was no real money at stake. He laughed. "Well played, Craig. Well played."

He began to organise the chips back into neat bundles.

"I think it's a great way to see a man's character; his

poker face tells you a lot about who the man really is. Do you fancy another game with something more solid at stake?" he asked with a strained smile.

The drilling in my head was replaced with the klaxon sound of an alarm.

"Eh, no, thanks. Can we get to that friendly chat you mentioned?"

"You're always in such a hurry, Craig. It's not good for your stress levels, you know. Your rushed judgement can also cause other people stress. For example, I believe you rushed to the conclusion that the recent unfortunate deaths connected with The Butterfly Collectors had something to do with my organisation. That, I'm afraid, affected my stress levels and my doctor has warned me about getting too tense it's not good for my heart, apparently."

"You're saying that these deaths have nothing to do with you?"

"Correct. Mr McAvoy was a good friend and business partner, why would I want him dead?" he asked simply.

I felt like I was treading close to a very dangerous trip wire. "Good friends and business partners have disagreements and fall out all the time."

"That is true but that is not what happened in this case. Mr McAvoy represents a major investment for my company and his loss will affect my business adversely."

He spoke like a legitimate businessman and I didn't

doubt that at some level he was but this was not it. Legitimate businessmen would not kidnap people to have a 'friendly' chat.

"Were you a major stakeholder in the agency?"

"You could call it that, yes."

"But if he suddenly came down with a dose of conscience, your stake would be very vulnerable. Vulnerable to the kind of scrutiny that might lead to your other business activities being shut down and you having to face some awkward questions from the police."

"That would have caused me problems, yes, had it happened, but it didn't."

I felt ridiculous dancing around the real essence of what he did but anything else exposed me to whatever other games he had planned.

"Who would have killed your good friend and why would they the kill the Jamiesons and the band's road manager?"

"I believe that my competitors may have killed Kris as a way of disrupting my business. Mr McEwan was another important asset to me at one time and the Jamiesons were collateral damage. The chance of a reunion for the band died with Ben, another way to have a negative affect on my investment."

"Because the band were such an important part of your portfolio?" I failed to keep the sarcastic tone from my voice.

"My father played an important part in getting

them started. We deserved to get something back on our investment, don't you think? A reunion tour and maybe a new record could have been very lucrative for my company."

"I think I know the important part your connections played in getting the band that first tour. It still seems a stretch to me. The three people associated with the band who were most involved with your illegal business are all dead. You've already said that you can't control your people as well as you would like. What if one of them decided on a little private enterprise? Maybe they fancied cutting out the middle man and getting their hands on that part of your business to build their own little empire, it's one possibility."

"Don't push the boundaries of my hospitality, Craig," he growled a warning.

"My people had absolutely nothing to do with this. Their loyalty is never in question because the consequences of betraying me would be dire for them and their families. You are looking in the wrong place because you don't understand how my organisation works. I think you should consider an alternative, and I think I can help to put you back on the right track. Our rivals recently had one of their men released from prison on a technicality. He is very adept with a gun, in fact I would go as far as to say he is an assassin. If there was anyone worth looking at, he's your man."

"You'd be willing to give me his name?" I asked

doubtfully.

He laughed. "No, there is a certain code that I must live by and that means I couldn't do that, but the police will be aware of this gentleman, I'm sure."

"Your code seems a little flexible. You could be playing me to try and get this guy back in jail, as an inconvenience to your rival."

"It's your right to think that, Craig but I assure you that there is no one in my organisation responsible for this and I believe that he is your best bet." He held my gaze with the frightening intensity of a man who does not like to be questioned.

"I'll pass on the information to the relevant authorities but it'll be hard to sell it, based on your word alone."

"That's all I can ask. Now I think it's time for you to go." He waved a hand and his son reached to grab me by the arm.

"It's OK. I can walk." I stood up and was glad that he was close enough to catch me as the room spun around me like I was sitting on a fairground ride.

"Thanks for the game, Craig. Maybe we'll play again some day." He said with a cheerful smile.

"I hope not," I muttered under my breath as I was led away.

A door opened into a large space that looked like an old warehouse or factory. There was a black van parked beside the door, and I was half dragged around to the back and then bundled roughly into it.

A wooden partition separated me from the cabin and the windows in the back were completely blacked out. I sat on the floor as there were no seats and I was bounced around, which did nothing for my head or my stomach. I could feel the pounding in my skull grow more intense and I struggled not to vomit.

The van travelled for about twenty-five minutes before I was dropped off back at my office. One of McGavigan's men threw my helmet and bag out of the van before they left.

I staggered as I walked to the bike and knew I wouldn't be able to ride it. I called Li and he agreed to come and help me. Before he arrived, my stomach gave up its contents into a drain and I slumped against a lamppost.

He arrived twenty minutes after I called and parked his car close to me. He was out and on the way over to me almost before his engine had stopped.

"Craig, what the hell happened?"

I tried to lift my head but the effort was too much. "Mugged," I managed to say, but it was difficult as the messages between my mouth and my brain seemed to be going via a satellite.

"I'll phone an ambulance." Li was dialling the phone before I could stop him. There were going to be awkward questions if I went to the hospital, questions I didn't want to answer. I tried to say no but I didn't quite manage it as I slumped from my resting place and followed the white rabbit down the black hole again.

***

I awoke with a bright light being shone in my eyes.

There was another period of disorientation and lack of focus before I could see the doctor who had been moving a torch across my eyes as she assessed my condition.

"Back with us Mr Campbell, that's good."

I tried to reply but my tongue was stuck to the roof of my mouth.

"John, can you get me some water?" she said to someone else in the room.

A short time later a male nurse held a cup to my lips and poured a little water into my mouth. It lubricated my tongue and I could feel it chilling its way down my throat.

"You've been in the wars. I need to ask you a few questions Mr Campbell. Do you think you can answer them?"

"Think so," I managed to say through my confusion.

"Can you tell me your full name?"

"Craig Kenneth Campbell"

"Do you know what month it is?"

"November."

"Who is the Prime Minister?"

"Cameron."

"That's good. There's no fracture but you do have a severe concussion. We'll keep you in overnight for observation."

I wanted to protest but knew I would be wasting my breath. I willingly gave in to sleep once more.

The next time I awoke Carol was sitting beside me, dozing.

"Hello," I said.

She roused herself and looked at me. There was a pause and then she hit me on the arm.

"You idiot." Then she burst into tears and leaned over to hug me.

We had a long conversation about how stupid I was and she lectured me for calling Li rather than her. I tried to defend myself but knew that she was right. She told me that my mum was on her way from Arbroath, which meant that I would be in for another lecture about my foolishness. In the middle of our conversation the door swung open and Alex walked in. I groaned and wished I was asleep.

"Hi Alex." Carol stood and hugged her. The forces of womanhood were allying against me.

"I'll go and get a tea, leave you to deal with this clown," Carol said before she walked out, abandoning me to the attentions of an angry policewoman.

"Do you want to tell me what happened? And don't spin me the 'I was mugged' bollocks you told the medical staff."

"Technically I told Li. Not even a bunch of grapes and a 'how are you?', Alex?" I said in an effort to inject some humour. Her stony face told me that I had maybe not caught the right mood.

"It amazes me how much of a complete fuckwit you can be." Alex wasn't someone who swore often. When she did it was normally at me and carried a considerable amount of weight.

"Look this isn't entirely my fault. I was ready to walk away, I was kind of pulled back in against my will. I even sent you an e-mail," I protested.

She shook her head. "Just tell me what happened and stop fannying about."

"I went to see Nancy Young, the girl that worked for McAvoy. Turns out she's Malcolm McGavigan's niece. She was planted in the agency to keep an eye on McAvoy, probably because McGavigan was worried McAvoy was getting cold feet about their business arrangement."

She looked puzzled. "What business arrangement?"

I then recited everything that Innes McEwan had told me about the band, McAvoy and the drugs.

Her surprise was genuine and it was obvious she had not guessed at the depth of the connection between McGavigan and the agency. "And you thought that it was something you should keep to yourself?"

"No. I was going to phone you tonight and leave it with you, honest. I had a mail prepared and everything."

"Craig, now is not a good time to lie to me."

"Honest. I can't play with these kinds of people, I know that. I was ready to give in when McGavigan's boys decided that they needed to reshape my head before taking me to meet their boss."

"Wait, you saw McGavigan?"

"Oh yes. He wanted to have 'friendly chat' as he put it. I played poker with him and he was keen to advise me where I was going wrong."

"Can you identify his thugs?"

"One of them was his son but I'm not even thinking of pressing charges. You know as well as I do that they'll have alibis that will put them in Edinburgh or Los Angeles if they want. McGavigan will have his lawyers claiming police persecution before you've finished your first question."

"I know." She was resigned to the force's impotence in the face of McGavigan and his cronies.

"So what did he want to speak to you about?" she asked.

"Well, first we had a surreal game of poker. He said that it was a good way to judge a man's character. Then he told me that he had nothing to do with the murders. McAvoy was a valued business partner and he had no reason to kill him. He then pointed me in the direction of one of his rival's men. Some guy with a history of gun crime who had been released recently due to some technicality. He reckoned that you should be looking at him."

"Did he mention any names?"

"No, he seemed to be sure that you would know who to look for."

"Did he say why he thought this guy would be the killer?"

"He said that it was a way for his rival to disrupt his business. He talked like he was importing toys or something. I think he believes he's a legitimate businessman."

"They're all the same when they get to his level. Delusional. Do you know where they took you?"

"No. It looked like a warehouse or a factory but they threw me in the back of a van with blacked-out windows on the way back and I was unconscious on the way there."

"Anything else that slipped your mind or that you decided not to tell me?" she said her voice swimming in sarcasm.

"Rebecca Marsh, the band's biographer, said that there was a threatening letter sent to the band in the wake of the fan's death. You know just before they split?"

She nodded.

"The letter mentioned McAvoy by name and said that he would be the first to die. She reckons it might be in the police records. It might be worth another look."

"Right, thanks. Now you promise that you'll leave

the rest to us."

"You bet."

"I'll pop round to see you tomorrow."

"Cheers."

She said goodbye and walked away as Carol returned. It was just the two of us again and I spent about an hour trying to convince my sceptical girlfriend that I was finished with the case.

CHAPTER THIRTEEN

I was released from hospital later that day. Carol drove me home and I noticed my bike in its usual spot outside our building. I made a mental note to thank Li.

When Carol opened the door to the flat, a welcoming smell of fresh coffee rolled out to greet us. I walked into the living room and standing in the kitchen was my mother. She rushed over and hugged me with the strength of a professional wrestler.

"Mum, you didn't need to come down."

"I'm your mother, where else was I meant to be?"

"I'm fine. It's just a bump on the head."

"Let's hope it knocked some sense into you," she said with the angry concern that only a parent can show.

"That's me. I'm out. No more investigating murders."

"Aye, well, it better be."

She walked back into the kitchen to attend to the coffee and prepare some scones, which she then delivered to the table.

The three of us sat drinking and eating, chatting about Mum's life in Arbroath.

She was still not entirely herself. I couldn't work out what had happened but ever since we found the baby's skeleton the previous year she had seemed distracted and disturbed. I thought that when I felt a bit better I would try to find out why it had affected her so much.

After about an hour I found myself drifting off to sleep and Carol ordered me to bed. I obeyed and left the pair of them talking.

***

The following day was Friday and it dawned with a watery sunshine. Carol had already gone to work by the time I roused myself. Mum was nowhere to be seen and I thought that she may have gone out shopping.

I finished my morning cleaning routine and fed myself with a bowl of porridge. My head was still aching but a couple of pills helped to alleviate it.

With little else to do I thought I would check what had been going on in the world while I was in hospital. I flopped down on the sofa with my computer on my lap. I loaded the browser and checked the BBC news site. An article in the Scottish news section caught my eye,

Police shooting in South Lanarkshire
I clicked on the link and the story was revealed.

'Strathclyde Police have confirmed that a suspect was killed in an incident in the Rutherglen, South Lanarkshire in the early hours of Friday morning.

Armed officers were called to the scene after a detective was shot and injured when he went to question the suspect in relation to unspecified crime.

Chief Superintendent Liam Derrick said: "A 32 year-old man was shot and killed by armed officers in Rutherglen at around 6 am. He had opened fire on two detectives when they went to question him about a routine matter. One of the detectives was injured.

The armed response unit was dispatched immediately. On arrival the officers tried to persuade the man to give himself up but after a short time he fired on them. They returned fire as per protocol and unfortunately the man was killed."

The officer indicated that there would be a full inquiry into what happened but is confident that his officers acted in a professional manner. He also said the injured detective was in a stable condition in the Royal Infirmary.

I wondered if the information I had given Alex the previous day had ended in the shootout. It could be a coincidence but there seemed to be a good chance that the man was involved in the shooting was also the gangland assassin. There was a sense of relief, and at least Carla would have some peace, if he was the killer. I thought about giving Alex a ring but she had said that she would be visiting me later so I decided against it.

I closed the computer and wondered what to do next. The biography of the band on the bookcase caught my eye and I decided to finish it for my own curiosity as much as anything else. I flicked through the pages until I found the part about the band's final album and Ben's brush with the law.

Hallowed ground

The band took a four-month break before they hit the studio again to record their fifth album, 'The Life & Times of The Sonic Rustler' in the spring of 2001.

The album was to be recorded in the hallowed environs of the famous Abbey Road studios in London. Ben was desperate to work in the room that had been home to The Beatles throughout their recording career and the rest of the band shared his enthusiasm.

The record was produced by Glenn Berkeley, a Californian with a background producing some of the leading R&B artists in his home country. The band had met him during a visit to Los Angeles the previous year. He had been enthusiastic about their music and had expressed an interest in working with them as he had never before produced rock artists.

As the band had gradually expanded their use of loops on the previous album, they were ready to diversify the type of musical sounds they used and to try to get a more expansive sound for the next release. Glenn offered an opportunity to push their music in a new and exciting direction. At a band meeting they were analytical in the decision about whether to work with the Californian. Jim Harris used a flip chart as they listed all the pros and cons of taking the leap of changing producer after four successful albums. In the end the pros outweighed the cons by a long way; only the risk of alienating their fans was seen as a major obstacle. They called Berkeley and he agreed to join the project.

The first day of recording was on March 22nd. Ben's rollercoaster use of drugs was thankfully on a trough and the only thing he was using was an occasional joint or a few beers. They were like kids in Disneyland as they were given a tour of the most famous recording studio in the world. They even took a photograph of the four of them walking across the world's most recognisable zebra crossing.

The session began with Ben singing a basic version of each song with a simple accompaniment by Jim. These were to be reference tracks only and were to provide the basic skeleton for the completed songs.

Glenn suggested that they try some of the songs at a different speed or a different tempo. He suggested that they try to expand their horizons by borrowing rhythms from Reggae or Latin or Jazz. Mark sat in and tapped out those rhythms on Jim's guitar case while Kenny watched and thought about what he would add. The session lasted twelve hours but the time passed quickly as the band enjoyed this new approach. When it was finished they had around eighteen different recordings of six different songs. The following two days were very similar and by the end of the third day they had sixty recordings of fifteen possible tracks for the album.

A day was spent narrowing down the list of tracks to work from before the serious business of recording the final tracks began. There was some debate between the band and the producer but slowly the band began to understand what Glenn was trying to do. He was introducing a new level of musical subtlety while keeping the basic essence of the band's sound intact.

After the versions of the tracks they were going to record were decided, the real sessions began. Glenn decided that the band weren't all required to be in the studio at the same time. He preferred to work with the drum and bass section first, to pin down the rhythm that would be the most important part of driving the songs. Jim and Ben weren't required and although Jim reported every day he soon became bored and Glenn suggested he go and try out some new guitars and effects pedals that they might use when it was time to add his riffs.

As Ben would be the last one to be involved he

would have the longest time to wait. Ben was never good with too much time on his hands and he was soon inviting friends round to his London flat which was just off King's Road in Chelsea. It didn't take long for quiet evenings to become wild parties. Some of those parties turned into events that lasted for three days. There was no shortage of either drink or drugs for the willing party-goers. The rest of the band knew nothing about how the singer was spending his free time as they were so captivated by the work they were doing.

Two weeks into the recording session Jim was called back to the studio to begin some of the guitar and keyboard pieces. They were only two hours into the session when the news came through.

At five-thirty that morning, twelve police officers had raided Ben's flat. The officers found people in every room in a variety of states of undress. Six were arrested for possession of a class A drug, including The Butterfly Collectors singer. They were taken to Chelsea police station and charged.

Kris McAvoy rushed down from Glasgow to sort out the mess. It was the first time that Ben had been arrested in relation to drugs and McAvoy was quick to get a top QC involved. Fortunately, it was the last day of a three-day binge and there was only a small amount of cocaine left in the flat. There was no chance he would be charged with intent to supply but McAvoy knew that the police would try to find a way to upgrade the charge if they could. The QC argued the case well and Ben was released on bail with a trial date set for June.

The press had known about Ben's drug habit for a while but there had been very little reported due to a lack of evidence and some clever press management by McAvoy. After the arrest, the tabloids went into overdrive as exaggerated stories of the parties were published. Ben's friends were all too keen to take their thirty pieces of silver from the journalists who were desperate for details more lurid than those published by rival publications. In some ways this worked in Ben's favour as the more details that the newspapers published, the more the possibility arose that he would not get a fair trial.

McAvoy decided to get Ben out of London until he was needed in the studio. He rented a cottage in the Cotswolds, which was the most remote that he could find. A crew of security guards was hired to prevent press intrusion. Ben was ordered not to leave and visitors were vetted by McAvoy before being allowed to see him.

Meanwhile, the other band members had continued to work on the album throughout the drama and the adverse publicity. The three musician were furious but there was nothing they could do but keep working.

Reporters camped on Abbey Road, eagerly hoping to get an interview with anyone connected with the band. They even tried questioning some members of the London Philharmonic Orchestra who were in another studio recording a film soundtrack.

Jim and Mark were particularly angry with their bandmate but no one would have guessed it from the united public face they projected. They appeared supportive and insisted that the band were fully behind their singer and that they would help him to move on from the incident.

The interest in the band's affairs eased when the press attention drifted to a Premiership footballer who had been caught in bed with a prostitute. Ben was back in London within three weeks of the police raid. He stayed at the home of a record company executive and was ferried to and from the studio like an errant schoolboy.

All the band's initial contributions to the songs were finished six weeks after the drugs incident. Ben was supervised constantly by at least one person during that time to ensure that there was no repeat of the trouble he had caused.

When the trial began Ben pled guilty to the charge of possession and was given a three-month community order and a six-month custodial sentence suspended for one year. The QC had argued against a custodial sentence due to it being Ben's first offence. However, the judge was not persuaded by the arguments although a suspended sentence was at least half a victory.

The scandal of the footballer had exploded into confessions of orgies and was more interesting to the more salacious members of the press. This meant that the trial received less coverage than it might have done and the damage to the band's reputation was minimal.

The recording sessions were due to move to Glenn's hometown of Los Angeles in July but once again Ben's legal troubles had caused problems for the band. Ben was refused a visa for the US due to the conviction. Kris McAvoy had to move quickly to secure a new venue and a studio in the south of France was found.

The band moved en masse to the French countryside to oversee the recording process as additional instruments and layered loops were added to their own contributions. Glenn wanted to expand their sound and he consulted them through every remix and recording as the sessions continued. The musicians he recruited offered the four band members a rare chance to expand their musical knowledge; Mark was particularly fascinated by a Moroccan percussionist who taught him a lot about Arabian music.

For the duration of the trip the band were housed in a converted farmhouse while they helped Glenn to create their new sound. Kenny had learned to play keyboards and his skills were put to use in that capacity for the first time, which he found both challenging and enjoyable.

At the height of the warm French summer the first track, 'Complications' was finished. Its beautiful melody was complemented by the rich textures of sound that enveloped it. Ben re-recorded his vocals and added a new dimension and emotion to his singing that matched the new sound. The other band members couldn't help being captivated by his performance and a little of the rift was healed again.

France proved to be the perfect place for him as his wife and young daughter had joined up with the group for the last two weeks. He re-recorded every vocal track with a level of emotional maturity and vocal dexterity that he had never achieved before. Recording was finished by the end of August and by the end of September the album was complete.

When the record company people flew in to hear it, a silence fell over the room. The band looked on nervously but there was no need for anxiety. All the staff from London were delighted and words like masterpiece and classic were used to describe what they heard. They brought forward the release from January of the following year to November 13th. It was to prove an inauspicious day.

CHAPTER FOURTEEN

I turned to the next page but my reading was interrupted by the chime of the doorbell. "Hello," I said into the intercom.

"Hi, Craig. It's Alex."

"Hi Alex, in you come." I buzzed her in to the building and moved to the kitchen to put on the kettle.

When I opened the door she greeted me with a gentle, tentative hug.

"How are you?"

"Apart from a lumpy head, I'm fine."

She sat in the living room while I prepared the coffee. A love of caffeine was one of the things that had drawn us together back in our university days.

She expressed her pleasure at the quality of the coffee before she said, "I've got some news for you."

"The shooting?" I asked as the investigator in me resurfaced.

"Yip. We think we've got him. I checked out the tip that McGavigan gave you. The guy's name was Lenny Christian and a more inappropriate surname you could not imagine. He crawled his way out of the slime using his fists to move up the ladder of the Carmichael organisation. He had a particular fondness for torture before developing a passion for guns. We reckon he was part of a gun running operation back in the eighties that the Carmichael clan ran for the UDA. He was jailed back in 2008 for his part in a particularly vicious knee-capping of an overambitious drug dealer in Castlemilk. The conviction was quashed in May when the prosecution's key witness was proved to be in another part of the city on the date of the assault. We know it was him but he walked and was even due compensation." I could read the frustration on her face. The police worked hard to put the villains away but the lawyers were always working an angle to get them out again.

"So what happened this morning?"

"A DS and DC from London Road were sent to bring him in for questioning about the band murders. They were supposed to wait for armed officers but somebody made a balls of it and they were sent out half an hour before they were supposed to. The DS decided to try to lift Christian before the armed team arrived, they were only bringing him for questioning. They chapped the door, identified themselves and told him that he was required to go with them. The DC was shot in the leg when Christian went mental. I heard he was screaming that he wasn't going back to prison and that no one would make him."

"How's the officer?"

"Fine, from what I've heard. He'll be getting physio for a while as the bullet shattered his femur, but he should make a full recovery. Anyway, when the armed team arrived, Christian began to take pot shots at them. Any attempt to talk to him was met with more gunfire. The chief super had no option but to order them to shoot. Ironically, a sniper shot Christian in the head after about twenty minutes of him shooting at the police."

"Bloody hell, sounds more like LA than Glasgow."

"When our lot eventually got into the flat they found an arms cache that any gangster in LA would have been proud of. He had automatic pistols, rifles and shotguns. Forensics are confident that one of them will be a match to the gun that killed the band. They discovered a ballistics match from the Collectors murders to a bullet used in an execution that the Carmichaels were believed to have committed in Maryhill a few years back. Christian was the most likely shooter, so we're hoping we'll find the gun in his collection. We're also putting out feelers to McGavigan to see if his lot have more information about the shootings."

I considered what Alex had told me. "Are you sure about this? We've only got McGavigan's word that this guy was involved."

"I know. But Christian's reaction was so extreme that it looks pretty suspicious, the ballistics is pretty strong evidence as well," she asserted.

"An arms cache might have been enough for him to react like that, though, don't you think? And it sounds like he had a real aversion to being locked up."

She sighed. "God, Craig, I thought you would be happy."

"If it was him, I will be. I don't think it's as cut and dried as I would have hoped for."

"We'll do our job."

It felt like I had annoyed Alex again with my scepticism but I believed it was all too convenient for McGavigan for all this to be wrapped up in a nice parcel with Christian's death being the bow on the top. It would be a major blow to the Carmichael organisation to lose a guy like Christian. I had to admit the news of the ballistics match was positive but McGavigan's crew could even have been behind the other murder.

I offered a conciliatory thought. "Let's hope you find that gun and Carla will be able to see that justice has been done for her folks."

The conversation turned to other things while Alex finished her coffee. I began to feel exhausted from the strains of the past few days and she realised that I was in need of some rest. She said her farewell and let herself out while I went back to bed.

***

When I woke up again it was dark outside and another storm was howling outside the apartment. I couldn't remember a time when we had so many storms battering the city in such a short space of time.

I roused myself and shambled through to the living room where Carol and my mother were sitting side-by-side. Carol was holding Mum's hand. Both their faces were streaked with tears.

My thoughts were still a little fuzzy and I couldn't imagine what could be wrong.

"What's up?"

Carol turned to me. "Your mum has something to tell you."

"Mum, what is it?"

She started to sob and my confusion deepened. I stepped toward her and Carol moved to allow me to sit next to Mum. I took her in my arms and she wailed into my shoulder, her sorrow, too strong for words.

After about ten minutes she seemed to calm a little and began to speak.

"Craig, I've been keeping a secret from you for far too long and I shouldn't have. I think it's time to let it go."

"What is it?" I couldn't imagine what could be so bad that she would react like this.

"You had a sister."

My pounding head and befuddled brain couldn't

quite get to grips with what she was saying.

"What?"

"You had a sister. Well, a stepsister."

"Mum, what are you talking about?"

"I had a baby, before I met your dad. She was still-born." The sobs began again.

Suddenly her reaction to our tragic find of the previous year made sense. All the pain, remorse and misery of that time in her own life had overwhelmed her. I hugged her tightly and tried to come to terms with what she had said. I made placating sounds as I calmed her and encouraged her to tell me the full story.

Eventually she stilled and began to talk again. "I met a married man about three years before I fell in love with your father. I was only eighteen and he seemed to be so mature and sophisticated. I thought I was in love with him and he with me. When I fell pregnant he told me he never wanted to see me again and that I was never to tell anyone. He tried to make me have an abortion at some backstreet dive but I couldn't go through with it. I never told a soul he was the father and I carried the baby to full term. She was a breach birth and the cord got wrapped around her neck. The midwives and doctors did all they could for her but she died before they could free her."

I sat with her in my arms, feeling shocked and desperately useless. I could not think what to say to this woman who had been my strength for so long.

She continued her tale. "She's buried in Maryhill cemetery. I have never told anyone what happened, I have never even visited the grave." She howled again and this time buried her face in her hands as if she was too ashamed to look at me. The sorrow radiated from her and I could feel it as my body reacted to her pain.

I looked at Carol and realised that Mum felt she could tell her before she could bring herself to tell me. A silence settled on the room like a blanket of melancholy. I couldn't understand why Mum had kept this to herself over all these years. That she hadn't been able to tell dad before he died was incredible. Why would anyone keep that amount of pain secreted away, hidden from the world as it ate away at her? The distress of finding the little body last year must have cut through the layers of secrecy like a laser, exposing all the anguish she had bottled up but still she had resisted telling me.

Rather than try to deal with my own emotions I decided to offer a practical short-term solution. "We'll go to the grave tomorrow and take some flowers. It's important that we acknowledge her."

She looked up. "Yes, I'd like that."

I could see Carol looking intently at me. She would have more to say later as she knew I was simply avoiding my own emotional needs. In truth I was ignoring my mother's as well.

We didn't speak about it for the rest of the evening, although Carol did try to prise a more considered reaction from me when Mum had gone to bed. I couldn't get my thoughts in any kind of order and told Carol as much.

***

The following morning we drove in Carol's car to the cemetery in the north of the city. On the way we stopped at a florists to pick up some flowers.

After we parked the car it took us a while to find the humble headstone.

Amanda MacPherson
Died 17th April, 1971

MacPherson was my mother's maiden name. We laid flowers and stood for a short while, each of us contemplating our own feelings and thoughts. I wondered what it would have been like to grow up with an older sister and what she would be doing now. There was also the slightly disquieting realisation that I might not have been here had she survived, it was a strange thought.

We drove to a restaurant and ate a simple lunch. Mum began to open up about how she had dealt with Amanda's death over the forty years of harbouring her secret. She felt that she had been punished for her affair and for not really wanting the baby. There was also a little piece of her that was scared of the baby's father and what he might have done had the baby survived.

I expressed my dismay that she hadn't told me earlier and both Carol and I reassured her that she had nothing to feel guilty about other than keeping the story to herself.

The conversation drew us all closer as a family. By the time lunch was over I could see glimpses of the mother I knew so well was beginning to return as the terrible weight of forty years began to lift.

She pressed me to find out if I was all right. I told her I was fine and she decided to head home the next day. I sought reassurances from her that she would tell her friends in Arbroath all that she had revealed in the past couple of days. I wanted her to have a support network on hand for the days she felt the grief creep up on her again. She guaranteed that she would tell them everything she had told me and I hoped she would be true to her word.

We returned to the flat a happier group than the one who had left earlier that morning.

***

On the Sunday morning, we drove Mum to Queen Street station through the quiescent city streets. Our parting on the platform was more emotional than normal but I was relieved to see that there were signs that Mum was getting back to her old self.

On the drive home, Carol began to gently gauge my emotions regarding the revelation.

"Now, Mr Campbell, are you reay to let that West of Scotland man facade drop and tell me what you're thinking?"

I looked across at her from the passenger seat. "I don't know, to be honest. It was a lot to take in. I'll get back to you." I smiled but Carol wasn't impressed.

"You're a hopeless case but I'm here whenever you're ready."

"I know." I laid a hand on hers and gave it a gentle squeeze. "What caused Mum to open up to you in the first place?"

"I asked her how Mrs Gilbert was doing after everything that happened. It was like a dam burst, she started crying and then she told me the full story."

We had found the baby's skeleton when I was trying to find Mrs Gilbert's cat. I didn't realise at the time how personal the find was for my mother and it was only now that reason for her reaction became clear.

"Why do you think she chose to tell you rather than me?"

"I don't know, love. Maybe she just needed to talk to a woman. Does it annoy you?"

"A little. I'm more annoyed she didn't think she could tell my father before he died. That feels like a betrayal somehow."

"It was difficult for her, she was embarrassed. They were different times, Craig."

"I know. I need a bit of time to adjust, that's all."

I had not yet shaken off the effects of McGavigans attentions and when we returned to the flat I needed some more rest.

I lay in bed and scanned the newspapers. There was a small piece about Innes McEwan's funeral. It was scheduled for the following day at the crematorium which is situated in the same cemetery in Maryhill I had been in the day before. I had felt sorry for Innes when I met him and decided to go along. I didn't think that there would be many in attendance.

***

The following day I dressed in my only black suit, white shirt and black tie. I covered it with the my waterproofs and set off.

When I reached the bike I pushed the helmet on to my head and received a sharp reminder that I was still sporting a considerable lump and plenty of bruising on my tender skull. I brushed away the worries of concussion and warnings about operating machinery that the doctor had emphasised before I left the hospital.

The service was held at nine-thirty on the Monday morning. As I passed through the gates I was surprised to see that the car park was nearly full. I left the bike beside a BMW, removed my biker clothing and packed it into the box at the back of the Ducati. I walked up the small hill to the red sandstone crematorium. There were already people milling about outside but there was no sign of the funeral cortege.

The congregation gravitated together to form small groups, talking quietly, mindful of the occasion.

While I waited, I looked at the flowers that were placed on the wet ground outside the building. I noticed wreaths from the management teams of both the Stones and U2, as well as more personal tributes from other bands. Innes had obviously made an impression during his time on the road.

About ten minutes after I had arrived the hearse moved slowly up the short drive towards us. There was a small convoy of cars behind it, some of them peeled away to find a spot in the car park while the family limousine followed the hearse to the door of the crematorium. The coffin was carried up the steps into the building by six men. Four of them looked like they were maybe colleagues from the music business and a couple seemed to be family members. They were followed by a two elderly ladies who looked enough alike for me to think they were sisters.

I joined the rest of the congregation as we filed into the entrance at the back of the small chapel. I nodded to the remaining members of the band as they took their place. Jim and Kenny were accompanied by their partners, Mark was on his own. Sandra Brown was there with Henry. She was dressed in an immaculate raven black suit. Her face was partially covered by a veil that fell from the edge of her hat. She looked more like a grieving widow than a casual acquaintance. Henry was less formal in a black shirt and black jeans.

The chapel was nearly full by the time the service began. The interior of the building was appropriate for both religious and humanist services. The service was conducted by a priest in conjunction with one of Innes McEwan's cousins. The two elderly ladies at the front were his aunts. The service consisted of passages from the Bible, one hymn and some tributes to Innes from former colleagues as well as a poignant personal tribute from Jim Harris on behalf of the band. It was the third funeral that they had attended in the space of a few weeks and it seemed to have taken its toll on the guitarist.

The priest thanked everyone for coming and on behalf of the family invited the congregation to join them at a local restaurant for the funeral meal. I had not planned to go but decided that as the band were all in attendance it would give me a chance to talk to them once again. I particularly wanted to talk to Jim Harris about his visit to Ben on the day he died. Despite the confidence Alex had that the killer had been found, I was still doubtful of the assassin theory and the stubborn bit of me was not going to rest until there was proof.

***

The restaurant the wake was held in was part of a chain, the bland decor the same as you would find in any of their establishments across the country. The staff had set aside an area for those who had attended the funeral.

The bar was already doing a roaring trade by the time I arrived. There were tables on one side, laid with a buffet of finger food as well as hot drinks. I helped myself to a surprisingly decent cup of coffee and waited while the band got some alcoholic drinks and settled at a table.

I walked to where they were seated and asked if I could join them. I was introduced to Jim's American partner, Cheryl Bailey and Kenny Strang's wife, Niamh.

There were moments of reflection and times when they shared some humorous reminiscences of Innes and their time on tour with him. Their warm feelings for those days and for their former roadie was obvious. I presumed that Mark must have been particularly close to Innes as he was very quiet, lost in his own thoughts.

As people began to leave, I asked Jim if I could have a word with him. We walked into a small room off the main function room.

"What's up?" he asked.

"Why didn't you tell me that you visited Ben on the day he died?"

"It wasn't important." He couldn't look me in the eye but it was difficult to decide if he was embarrassed or feeling guilty about something.

"You didn't think it was important that you were one of the last people to see your friend alive?"

"No."

"Did you tell the police?"

"No. It never came up."

"If I can find out you were there, so will they. Then they'll start thinking the way I am, that you have something to hide."

"I know, but honestly it's not important. I met him, we talked and when I left they were both alive."

"I don't understand why you are so defensive about this, tell me what happened."

"The conversation didn't end well. We argued about McAvoy. Ben told me he had suspicions about him and that he had hired you. I told him he should go to the police and then a lot of old crap got dragged up. I said some things that I shouldn't have and those were the last words I said to him. I feel like crap."

"Did he mention any concerns he had about McAvoy's drug connections?"

"I pressed him on it. I always believed that a lot of what we were owed was going into pockets other than McAvoy's. I didn't know for sure but I was convinced Ben did. He admitted to me that he was worried McAvoy was in too deep and that there were some heavy people behind him. I wouldn't let it go and eventually he admitted that he knew it was the McGavigan clan. Innes told him a while ago who they were but I had no idea that they were behind McAvoy. When Ben told me about the connection we really got into it and shouted insults at one another. Every little thing that had divided us was brought up and blown out of proportion. Like brothers, I suppose. Sad thing is I think he agreed with me, but he still had that strange loyalty to Kris that I never understood."

It all pointed to exactly what the police suspected, the whole thing was a gangland feud that had engulfed some innocent people. Probably because it was an easy way to create problems for McGavigan while ensuring that the warning from the Carmichael gang was clearly understood by the other warring faction.

"You didn't see anyone else when you were there?"

"No. I left in a hurry around five, I think it was."

Jim's regrets were obvious in his demeanour and I doubted that he was lying. The feeling that the case was at an end was the only sensible conclusion.

CHAPTER FIFTEEN

It was early afternoon when I returned to the flat. Carol was at work and it gave me some time to consider where my life was going.

My mother's revelations had caused me some mental distress but it was far from the only thing. The incident with McGavigan had shaken my confidence and there was now a big hole in my future.

The role of private detective had excited me but now it looked like a poor career choice. The thought of abandoning that role to return exclusively to mundane insurance work was not one I wanted to consider. The alternative was a change in career and the job market was hardly welcoming for anyone, never mind someone with my limited set of skills.

My musings were interrupted by the trilling of my phone. It was Rebecca Marsh. I was so far into the crater of my self-pity that I thought about ignoring it but I dismissed my own problems and decided to speak to her.

"Hi, Rebecca."

"Hi, Craig. Are you OK?" She had tuned into my unwillingness.

"I'm fine, just some aches and pains."

"Craig, I found a copy of that letter I was telling you about. I thought I had taken a photocopy when it looked like we were going to use it in the book."

"That's good," I said with as much enthusiasm as I could muster, which wasn't a great deal. "I don't know if it will be all that important; the police think they've found and dealt with the killer."

"Oh. Do you want me to send it over anyway? I can scan it and e-mail it so you can have a look."

I didn't want to appear ungrateful even though I wasn't likely to do anything with it. "That's fine, thank you."

"It'll be with you in five. It'll be informative if nothing else."

"Thanks, Rebecca."

She hung up and within a short time the mail application on my mobile phone showed that it had arrived. I left it on the phone; I would send an acknowledgement later.

***

I spent an hour restlessly trying to occupy myself. The TV, Playstation and radio proved to be useless at dispelling my negative thoughts. The bookcase called once more and I lifted Rebecca's book one last time.

Tragic End

As the release of 'Sonic Rustler' approached, Kris McAvoy decided to organise a special preview gig for members of the Collectors' fan club.

The first place he tried was King Tut's and by luck they had an opening on November 12th, the night before the album was due to be released. He sent out invitations to the first two hundred and fifty people who joined the fan club in the early days, the people who had supported the band from before they released their first album. The other spots were reserved for the music journalists from newspapers and magazines who would help to influence how well the album performed both critically and commercially.

Ben had been on his best behaviour since his arrest but everyone connected with the band knew that he was vulnerable on the run up to an album release. He was incapable of facing the pressure of letting the fans and press hear new work, as if the adulation would disappear overnight. He always expected the band's run of success to end and on previous occasions had turned to chemical support to get him through similar crucial days in the band's career.

McAvoy decided to manage the situation in an unusual way by allowing Ben to drink heavily on the 10th. The danger was that he would need more than Jim Beam or Southern Comfort to set him up for the big night but in the end a stinking hangover on the 11th was enough to at least control the singer's excesses.

The band assembled in a Glasgow rehearsal studio on the afternoon of the gig. There had been a lot of work done to replicate the sound of the album in a live environment. A Mancunian keyboard player called Taz McIlroy had joined the four-piece for the upcoming tour. For the initial gig, Glenn Berkeley was responsible for producing the looped tracks that were essential for the band's new sound. A laptop was set up to allow him to bring the significant contribution of the musicians that had joined the band in France.

Ben controlled his nerves and despite one or two minor problems the rehearsal went well. McAvoy looked on like a proud father as he realised that this was going to be their best work yet and that it would push them into the top echelons of the music business. He believed that critical acclaim was assured but there was still the slight concern about the fans' reaction. He hoped that this gig would be the first step in getting them on board.

After the rehearsal the newly expanded band line-up went to a city-centre hotel before heading to the gig later that night. Everyone kept an eye on Ben but his only intake was a bottle of beer.

They arrived at the venue forty-five minutes before the gig. The tiny dressing room did nothing to help release the tension they were feeling. The nervous chatter intensified before a strange quiet descended when they got the five minutes call; each member of the band had their own pre-gig routine, it was a time for personal preparations.

The plan was to play the album in its entirety, in the order the tracks appeared on the CD and then finish the gig with an encore of three hits. When they took to the stage the fans seemed to be as nervous as the musicians. The band had been drip-feeding the press with news on the run up to the release of the album. The crowd knew that they were about to be taken in a new direction by their favourites and were obviously worried that they wouldn't like it.

"We are worried about the reaction we will get. We believe in the new sound, but it's all going to be pointless if no one else tunes in to what we are trying to do," the lead singer told Q magazine in an interview he gave a few weeks before the release of the album.

The opening track was the upbeat 'Now Is The Time'. It was the closest thing they had to their old sound but it began to introduce the new ideas that had blossomed under Glenn's guiding hand. The lyrics were full of a buoyant hope that this was indeed the band's time to step into the top division of artists. The crowd, reserved at first gradually began to understand and enjoy what they were hearing. Their reaction seemed to intensify as the song progressed and Ben noticed some of the journalists nodding appreciatively when it was finished.

The rest of the set was received enthusiastically by

a rapturous crowd who seemed to realise they were attending a momentous event. When the band came back for the encore many of the fans were chanting for tracks they had just heard like 'Complications' and 'Real Difference'. After a short conference on the stage they reprised 'Complications' before finishing with the pre-arranged encores.

The band left the stage to enormous cheers and calls for another encore. It was a triumph and 'The Life and Times Of The Sonic Rustler' looked destined to be their magnum opus.

McAvoy was delirious. The really big money was beckoning as the band looked set to be a global phenomenon, it might even allow them to try to break America once again. He had organised an after-show party in a function suite of the hotel they had been earlier in the day. Everyone at the gig was invited back to celebrate the new album.

Glenn Berkeley volunteered to be the DJ for the party and his roots in R&B were obvious in the skilful way he mixed the tracks, even throwing in some of the Collectors' own tunes to the delight of the fans.

Nineteen-year-old Steven Parker had left his home in Falkirk to go to see his heroes debut their new album. A student at Strathclyde University, he was an accomplished musician in his own right, after being inspired to learn to play guitar by The Butterfly Collectors' music. He had dabbled with ecstasy at previous gigs and nights out with friends.

He bought a couple of tablets from a fellow student two days earlier in preparation for the concert. He took the first tablet a couple of hours before arriving at King Tut's. During the gig he drank six bottles of beer and when he reached the after-show party he felt the effects of the earlier dose were waning, so he decided to take the second tab.

At three o'clock in the morning a sudden shout from a corner of the hall brought the party to a shuddering halt. A young man had taken a fit and no one could rouse him despite a number of frantic efforts. An ambulance was called but before it could arrive his heart stopped.

The second tablet had proved to be too much for Stephen and he died in the hall with shocked fans looking on. The police were called and took the details of everyone in attendance. All the interviews were conducted over the following days but there was little that the fans added to help the investigation.

The band and their entourage were searched for drugs and interviewed at length. The recent publicity regarding Ben's drug habit made the officers very suspicious of him and the rest of the group. Some of the officers obviously believed that they were somehow involved in supplying Steven with the drugs. They were fortunate in that Kenny had decided not to indulge in his usual after-show joint and there were no drugs found on any of them or in their rooms.

The tragedy was the headline news in the

later editions of the morning papers, with many moralising before they knew all the facts. One of the more reactionary papers blamed the band and their culture of 'uninhibited drug use with no regard for the cost in human life'.

The band were devastated by what had happened. Ben felt the guilt most deeply and it would prove to be the catalyst for him to reject drugs completely.

There was nothing that could be done about the sale of the album as the CDs were already in stores. The release was obviously overshadowed by the death and some of the same newspapers called the band callous for allowing the album to be sold.

The media coverage hinted at all kinds of things and blindly ignored all that the police had to say on the matter. As a result of the moral crusade, the band received a number of threatening and insulting letters.

The post-mortem found that the second tablet proved to be too much for Steven who had an undiagnosed heart condition. The thorough police investigation found no connection to anyone in the band with regards to the drugs. It didn't stop some members of Steven's family joining in the campaign to blame them for the student's death.

The band were represented at Steven's funeral by Jim, Mark and Kris McAvoy. Ben had wanted to go but was unable to deal with it; the combination of the memories of his father's heart failure, the guilt over Steven's death and the media attention were too much for him to handle.

The Parker family had to endure a further tragedy when Steven's father, devastated by the loss of his son, took his own life just two weeks after Steven's death. Mark Davison attended the funeral despite concerns from the others that it would be inappropriate.

The pressure continued to mount on the band, who had already cancelled the tour that was meant to promote the release of the album. A meeting was called early in 2002 to discuss their future.

Ben had been receiving treatment for depression and was the first to suggest calling it a day. Kris McAvoy was horrified and tried to argue the case for continuing. He said that he wanted the album to be a tribute to Steven and even suggested a benefit gig for his family. Jim Harris could see through McAvoy's veil of concern and challenged him to be honest about his intentions.

Jim was disgusted by what had happened and felt that although they weren't directly to blame for the young fan's death, they did share some responsibility.

The other two band members knew that without Ben and Jim the band was finished and they tried to influence the decision but their arguments fell on deaf ears. Both Kenny and Mark could see that there was no changing their bandmates minds and eventually relented in their attempts to keep the band together.

The press release was published the following day.

'In light of recent events the members of The Butterfly Collectors have decided to bring the band to an end. They wish to convey their sincere sympathies to the family of Steven Parker. They also wish to express their thanks to the loyal fans who have shared this journey with them.'

It was a simple way to bring the tragic episode, and indeed their career, to an end.

There was another chapter in the book on what the band did after the split but I wasn't that interested and gave it a miss.

I flicked back through the pages to the photographs that are a standard part of most biographies. I never look at them while I'm reading a book as I find they interrupt the flow of the prose.

The first section had some photographs of the musicians as kids. Ben's Dad sitting proudly beside his son with the keyboard on Christmas Day. Jim aged about eight playing on Ayr beach. There was an early picture of the four of them not long after the band was formed, proudly displaying their instruments and their sense of camaraderie. There was a single grainy black-and-white photograph of Ben on the stage at King Tut's the night that they met McAvoy. The veins on his head and neck were prominent as he threw everything he had into the performance.

The next section dealt with their early career. Some of the images were the type of publicity shots that every band issues; serious looks, outlandish dress and ridiculous poses. The more interesting shots were the candid photos taken by Mark on an old SLR camera. They showed the warm relationship the band shared in the studio and on the road.

The final photographs were of the successful days of huge festival crowds and fantastic record sales. The last three pictures were the most poignant. The band arm in arm as they took their bow in front of the audience at their final gig at King Tuts. Then there were two pictures of the aftermath. Steven Parker's funeral and Kris McAvoy looking ashen-faced as he announced their demise.

I looked closely at the photograph of the funeral; it was a reprint of a shot from a newspaper. The members of the band in attendance were solemn and looked a little uncomfortable as if they felt they were intruding. At the front, among the leading mourners was a face I thought I recognised. A woman in her late twenties stood at the back of a small group. She had short, dark hair, her face a pale mask of grief, but there was something about her that looked familiar. I couldn't quite put my finger on it but there was definitely something about her.

The picture niggled at me for about fifteen minutes before I had a sudden inspiration. I had to check the letter that Rebecca had sent me.

I reached for my MacBook and booted it up. I found

the mail and loaded the scanned letter. A icy finger of suspicion pressed on me as I realised that I recognised the hand-writing and suddenly it all began to fit together.

I read the details of the letter.

'I know that Steven Parker's death was your fault. Your lifestyle has made young people believe that drugs are cool. You have ruined a family. I will avenge his death and show everyone that you are criminals.

It won't happen now but it will happen. Some day when you think you are safe. It'll be when you are sitting in your mansions enjoying your ill-gotten gains, it will be when you have forgotten all about that young man's death and all the promise that he had. It will be when you least expect it. You will never be safe from me. I promise.'

I tossed the computer aside and ran to search my wallet. I found the note that Sandra Brown had written for me, the one with the phone number of Nancy Young. I sat it beside the picture of the letter on the screen. She had written Nancy's name, address and phone number. There were enough similarities in the script to confirm my suspicions. Sandra Brown had written that deadly warning all those years ago.

I picked up the book again and looked at the woman in the picture. I was now convinced that it was McAvoy's employee and that she had some connection to Steven Parker. Now all I had to do was prove she was also a killer.

CHAPTER SIXTEEN

I reached for my phone and called Alex. It rang until her voicemail kicked in.

"Alex, phone me as soon as you get this message. I think I know who the real murderer is," I said with as much conviction as I could, hoping that she wouldn't ignore it as just a flight of fancy, a symptom of my injured skull.

I tried Jim Harris's number but once again was frustrated by the monotone of a voicemail message.

As my desperation rose, I tried Carla Jamieson. On the third ring she responded.

"Hi, Craig."

"Carla do you know if the band are at the rehearsal studios today?"

"No, Jim told me Sandra Brown had asked them to go to the concert hall this afternoon to finalise details for tomorrow night's show. He had asked me if I wanted to go down but I said no, I would leave it up to them. Why, what's up?"

I didn't want to alarm her so I said, "I've got a few more questions, that's all. I'll maybe pop over and catch them at the hall."

"OK, I'll speak to you later."

The call ended and I walked to our room to find my bike gear. I still hadn't cleaned any of it since the night Li had picked me up from the car park outside my office. Ignoring the dirt and dust, I pulled on the trousers and slipped into the jacket.

Outside, the sun was finishing its day's work and cast a crimson light across the city. The bike sat bathed in the light, its every surface looking like it was on fire.

The engine roared to life and I was off.

I tried to reassure myself that the remaining band members would be safe. I just needed to see it for myself and to tell them what I had discovered.

The beginning of the rush hour traffic slowed me slightly but within twenty minutes I was getting off the bike in the car park of the Buchanan Galleries. I placed the helmet in the storage compartment of the bike and began to run towards the concert hall.

***

The Glasgow Royal Concert Hall as it is formally known was opened in 1990. It is a substantial building clad in the same blonde sandstone that you can find in some of the city's tenements. It boasts an auditorium with acoustics as good as anything else in the country and is the home to orchestral performances, the Celtic Connections folk festival, and some rock shows.

I ran up the long steep steps to the entrance, pumping my legs as hard as I could.

The middle-aged man who was sitting behind the reception desk in the spacious foyer looked concerned as I approached.

"Can I help you... sir?" I imagined that I must have looked liked some lunatic biker in mucky clothes but I calmed my breathing and tried to compose myself and set my face to business mode.

"I'm Craig Campbell, I've been hired to look after the security of the remaining members of The Butterfly Collectors. I believe there may be a direct threat to them and would like to see them immediately."

"I'm sorry, sir. That won't be possible."

I reached into my jacket and flashed my private investigator licence at him.

"This could really be a matter of life and death, George," I said calmly as I read his name from his badge.

"We're under strict instructions that no one is allowed to see the band without prior permission." His jobsworth gene was kicking in.

"George, I'm not sure that you will look too clever if these guys are harmed because you decide that you have to follow the rules to the letter. I believe the person who killed their bandmate, manager and roadie is in this building and may be about to complete their work. The press will have a field day with you. Do you understand?" I conveyed my urgency and managed to keep my temper in check.

At the mention of the press I could see the panic and indecision settle on his face.

"They might still be on the stage, they were doing something about lights, I think. If not they'll be in the dressing room area finalising arrangements."

"George, you're a hero, thanks."

I ran through a sturdy set of doors to the large open area that housed a bar where people would congregate before a show and at the interval. I rushed past the patrons who had popped in for a coffee, getting some strange looks as I progressed through the room. I looked for the doors that would take me to the stalls. When I entered the auditorium the stage was dark and deserted; the only illumination came from emergency lighting. My running footsteps filled the space that has echoed to the sound of some of the biggest artists in the world.

I reached the platform and vaulted up on to it. The access to the stage is on the left as the audience look at it. I barged through the door and into a corridor. A simple sign pointed to the dressing room area. I followed a series of similar signs that directed me through a labyrinth of corridors and down some stairs.

I turned another corner and my worst fears were realised. Paul, the young technician I had met when I visited the rehearsal studio was lying in the corridor, his blood pooling in a large red pond around him. He had been shot in the shoulder. I had to check his pulse before I could continue my search for the band. My hand was covered in blood as I pulled it away. He was still alive but his pulse was weak and thready.

I tried a couple of doors before one gave way and swung open on to a nightmare. I didn't need to check their pulses to see that both Jim Harris and Kenny Strang were dead. A single bullet in each of their foreheads, their faces a frozen blue-white visage of lifelessness, limbs splayed like broken automatons. The dressing room mirrors were spattered with a thin film of brownish red blood, like some macabre Jackson Pollock picture. There was no sign of struggle; they had died trusting their killer.

I charged in to the remaining dressing rooms but there was no sign of Mark Davidson.

I rang the emergency services, detailing all that I had seen, urging them to get an ambulance as quickly as possible. As I finished the call my phone rang and Alex's name popped up on the screen.

"Alex, thank Christ. It's Sandra Brown, she's murdered both Harris and Strang. She's connected in some way to the young guy that died at the Collectors gig. I think it's all about revenge."

"Craig, where the hell are you?"

"I'm at the concert hall. Can you get someone to her house? She might have Mark Davidson as a hostage. I'm going to McAvoy's office in case she's there. I'll meet you there and please bring some friends."

"Craig, stay where you are. We'll deal with this."

"No, it might be too late." I hung up before she could say anymore.

I had noticed some towels in the dressing room that I quickly retrieved and pressed into service as improvised bandages for the young technician.

The race back to the foyer seemed longer than my trip down but when I reached George I gave him the briefest details of what had happened and asked him to go to be with Paul until the ambulance arrived. I told him that I would speak to the police when I was finished but that I had to try to catch the murderer. His suddenly grey face nodded a stunned agreement and I headed out into the street.

I had an internal debate but decided that going back to the bike would take too long. I barged my way through angry shoppers as I sprinted down Buchanan Street until I reached St Vincent Street. I burst through the door of the office building that housed McAvoy's agency and paused.

Now that I had reached my goal I had no idea what I would do if Brown was up there. She was obviously quite capable of killing me, she wouldn't give it a second thought. The best I could do was delay her until Alex and her colleagues arrived. I could only hope that Mark was still alive.

I ran up the thick stone stairs two at a time until I reached the outer office door. The lights of the office cast a yellow glow on to the murky landing. I stopped again, this time to listen at the door. There was a faint noise and then I heard a voice, but it seemed to be coming from McAvoy's inner room rather than the larger outer office. I gently eased down the handle and slowly edged the door open.

I could now hear a conversation and wondered if Brown was speaking to one of the other McAvoy employees, maybe she had an accomplice. I hunkered down and crept in to the room.

There was no one in the outer office and I reached the safety of the first desk. I crawled through the space under the desk until reached Brown's desk. I could now hear their exchange more clearly as the door was ajar.

"Why are ye daein' this?" a male voice that sounded like Mark Davidson but I could hear a tremor of fear in it.

"Shut up and pack that bag. I've got a flight to catch."

I could hear a sniff, he seemed to be crying. "They'll catch you, why no' jist gie yirsel up noo?" he pleaded.

"Don't talk to me like I'm an idiot. I've been planning this for ages. They think that guy in Rutherglen did it, they'll only find out it wasn't him when I'm long gone."

I quietly crawled forward so I could see into the office. I had a view of Mark Davidson's back. He was taking cash from a safe that was behind the large piece of office art I had noticed on my first visit to the agency. He was stuffing large bundles into a sports holdall. I could hear a rustling sound, and I presumed that Brown was going through some of McAvoy's papers.

I could see Mark's body was trembling with every movement. I moved back under Brown's desk, my heart was pounding and my head pulsed to the same beat.

I took out my phone and made sure it was on silent before I fired a quick text message to Alex. *'Brown, D'son at Mc Ofce. Hurry.'*

"That's aw the money. Ur ye gonnae kil me noo?" I could only imagine the depth of his fear.

"Shut up. Sit down with your hands behind your head." She dismissed him like he was a child.

"Please! Please! Don't kill me. Ah doan't want tae die."

"Be quiet or I'll be adding an extra hole to your head." There was an emotional detachment in her voice that was more terrifying than any threat or scream I had ever heard.

He was now sobbing uncontrollably, terrified that he was about to go the same way as his bandmates. I had no idea how I could help him.

"Got it," Brown shouted triumphantly. "Right, let's go." I could see her in the gap in the door with a bundle of papers that she threw into the holdall with the money.

"Up," she commanded.

"Oh God, oh God," Mark howled as he tried to stand. I could see that the fear had caused him to lose control of his body and the front of his trousers were stained with a patch of urine.

"Please, I don't want to die. Why ur ye daeing this? please tell me."

"You're not going to die as long as you do as I tell you. You're going to drive me to the airport and then you're going to wait two hours before contacting the police. I will know if you don't do as I say."

"But I came to your dad's funeral, we were all devastated by what happened to your brother. His death wasn't our fault."

"How dare you. He would never have taken those tablets if it wasn't for you lot. He idolised you. I was supposed to protect him but you stole him from me, he should be here now. You ruined our family. You would be dead by now if you hadn't come to my father's funeral, so unless you want me to change my mind you better do as I say. Move."

She gestured and I could see the gun in her hand. Mark picked up the bag, she tucked in behind him as he walked to the door

When they reached the frame of the door, I charged

from my hiding place bellowing with all the force of a charging elephant. I hit Mark's legs low, tackling him like a rugby player. He screamed in shock and pain as he crashed into Brown, who was directly behind him. The bag of money flew into the air and bundles of notes rained down across the office.

Having got that far I had no idea what to do next. I raised myself off his legs and before he could react tried to push him aside while I went after the killer.

Brown had managed to slide her legs out from under both of us. She looked for the gun that had been knocked from her hand by the force of our collision.

I pulled the bag from under me and tossed it at her to distract her from her goal.

Scrambling after Brown, I managed to catch her leg but she kicked out, the stiletto of her high heel catching me on the shoulder. My bike jacket prevented her from puncturing the skin but she must have hit a nerve as my left arm went numb.

I pushed off with my legs and propelled myself forward, my weight temporarily pinning her down. She began to wave her hand around under the desk, frantically trying to retrieve the weapon.

Eventually she pulled the gun from under McAvoy's chair, holding it by the barrel. I knew that I couldn't let her get a proper hold of the grip or I would be in trouble. I threw up my right hand and grabbed her upper arm and shook it. The gun came loose again and rattled across the floor before it skidded to a halt on the other side of the office.

She screamed and began to claw at my face, her nails like the talons of a raptor. I pushed further up her body and used my size to my advantage but she continued to rail and scratch like a trapped wildcat. One of her scratches caught my eyelid. It was enough to make me transfer my weight away from her and she wriggled free.

She scampered on all fours towards the gun. When she reached it, she turned to face me. She raised the pistol, staring down the barrel with a look of cold ambivalence.

I waited for the fatal shot but instead I heard a strong male voice shout, "Armed police."

At the sound of the officer's voice, some survival instinct must have kicked in. She lowered the gun before throwing it away to the other side of the room.

I looked up to see three officers edge into the room to secure both the gun and the prisoner.

Mark sat on the floor, his arms covered his head in a protective gesture that made him look like a small boy.

The ferocious vixen disappeared as she suddenly began to cry. As the police officer secured her hands she began to shout at me.

"Why? Why did you have to stick your nose in? They deserved to die, they killed my brother. My father killed himself because of them. They ruined the life of everyone in my family. They deserved to die."

I stood up and shook my head. I caught my breath. "No, Sandra, they didn't."

"They did. It's all their fault. He was a good kid. He would never have taken they drugs if he had never idolised those bastards." She screamed with force that caused her voice to crack.

There was a definite sadness that the events of ten years previously had resulted in so many deaths but I had to tell her the truth. "No, I'm sorry, you're wrong. You just can't face the fact that your brother made a wrong choice. Everyone has to take responsibility for their own decisions. Steven was naive or unlucky or both, but no one forced him to take those tablets. I can understand your father's hurt but he made the decision to leave you and your mother behind. And no one forced you to kill six people out of some misguided desire for revenge." I spoke quietly as the tragic nature of her delusion became apparent.

"Craig, you OK?" It was Alex, standing in the doorway taking in the scene as Brown continued to shout abuse at anyone within earshot but mainly in my direction.

"I'm good, and boy am I glad to see you."

"I thought you had quit the detecting game."

"I have, believe me, this was not in the plan."

She laughed and offered me a hand to help me up. Another officer went to help Mark, as yet another handcuffed Brown and roughly escorted her from the room. I breathed a sigh of relief.

EPILOGUE

The following day I was back in Ben Jamieson's white room with Carla and Alex who had asked me to accompany her.

"How are you?" I asked Carla when she had settled into her seat.

"A bit numb, I think. It's all been a bit too much to take in to be honest. I'm relieved it's over but so many people dead. It's just awful." She sighed.

"I can help with the details if you would like," Alex offered.

Carla considered her response before she replied, "Yes, I think I would. It might help to get it sorted out in my mind."

I was equally curious as to what the police had discovered from Ms Brown.

"As you'll have seen in today's papers, Sandra Brown is the sister of Steven Parker, the lad who died at the party back in 2001. She's been fixated with the belief that the death of her brother was as a result of his love of the band. The fact that her father committed suicide also contributed to how she reacted. She became obsessed and fixated on the band after the police investigation, she believed that it had been a whitewash and that the police were covering up the real story."

"She married Neil Brown in 2003 and moved to Houston with him, he worked in the oil industry. While she was in America she joined a gun club and became very adept with a pistol. Her husband was murdered in 2006. She claimed that two gunmen raided their home and that her husband was killed when he tried to stop them. I think the police in Houston will be taking a closer look at that in light of what has happened as the killers were never found."

"I'll bet they will," I observed.

"Her obsession only deepened during her time in the States and she was determined to avenge the death of her brother."

"When she came back to Scotland in 2007 she began investigating the band and McAvoy. She learned all she could about the music business, studying to perfect her cover. She managed to get a job in the agency and became McAvoy's personal assistant in 2009. It meant she had full access to all that was going on. She became McAvoy's confidant and learned how deeply he was in the pockets of the McGavigan clan.

That was the lever she needed to develop her plan."

Alex was warming to her task. "Like everyone else in the city she knew about the battle between Carmichael and McGavigan to supply drugs in the city. She is extremely resourceful and wormed her way to the top men in the Carmichael organisation. She told them all about the relationship between McAvoy and the McGavigans, told them everything. She knew about the smuggling and distribution and knew that it would harm McGavigan's plans if McAvoy was out of the picture. She told us that it took her a year to persuade the Carmichaels to trust her to do what she wanted. They supplied her with the gun."

"That is one very obsessed woman."

"You're right. To be honest I think she was probably a bit disturbed before her brother's death. The trauma probably tipped her over the edge."

"Why go to these lengths? She could have exposed McAvoy to the police," I said.

"Partly because she's unhinged. She has a deep mistrust of the force, they covered up her brother's death as far as she was concerned. Anyway that wouldn't have been enough for her, the band were her real fixation and revenge was all she really wanted."

"What will happen to her?"

"She'll go to prison. There's no lawyer will be able to get her out of this. She's confessed and the evidence is overwhelming." Alex sounded convinced that justice would be done.

"So what about Mark, why didn't she kill him?" Carla asked.

"Apparently he wrote to her in the wake of Steven's death. He also attended her dad's funeral. I think that memory earned him a reprieve but that's not to say that she wouldn't have killed him when they got to the airport."

"He's lucky to be alive but I have no idea how he's going to cope with all that has happened," I said.

"He'll need support and some strong people around him," Alex replied.

"We've both lost so much in such a short time." Carla whispered, reflecting the tough struggle she had in front of her. It would be particularly taxing for such a young woman.

"What are you going to do?" I asked.

"I'm selling the house and I'm going down to Birmingham to be near my grand parents. There are too many ghosts in this place, it is too big for me anyway."

"I hope you can make a fresh start."

"It might take time but I'm determined to do all that I can to keep their memory alive by living well and being happy. There's a lot of interest in the band, so maybe I can find something to help people remember how good they were," she stated with a firm conviction.

"I wish you the best of luck. We'd better be going." Alex said.

We walked to the front door but Carla stopped us. "Oh, Craig, before you go can you wait a moment?" She stepped back into the room we had just exited.

When she returned she was clutching the 1956 Gibson Les Paul Goldtop guitar.

"I would like you to have this, for all that you've done."

I was temporarily lost for words. "I...I can't accept this."

"Of course you can. I can think of no better home for it than with someone who loved Dad's music." She managed a smile that was laden with sadness. She placed the guitar in a sturdy touring case and handed it to me.

"Thank you. I will treasure it." I felt genuinely humbled by her gesture.

Alex and I hugged her in front of the house before we got into Alex's Mondeo.

As we drove down the tree-lined gravel, I glanced back at the lonely young woman as she waved from the door.

"So Mr Campbell, is that the life of a detective over for you?" Alex asked.

I thought for a moment. "We'll have to wait and see, Alex. Who knows?"

THE END

About The Author

Sinclair Macleod was born and raised in Glasgow. He worked in the railway industry for 23 years, the majority of which were in IT.

A lifelong love of mystery novels, including the classic American detectives of Hammett, Chandler and Ross Macdonald, inspired him to write his first novel, The Reluctant Detective. The Killer Performer is the third novel featuring Craig Campbell.

Sinclair lives in Bishopbriggs, just outside his native city with his wife, Kim and daughter, Kirsten.

For more information go to
www.reluctantdetective.com
twitter: @sinclairmacleod

Also Available by Sinclair Macleod

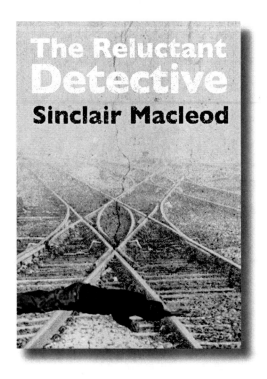

"I want you to find who killed my son."

Craig Campbell's quiet life as an insurance investigator is turned upside down when Ann Kilpatrick hires him to find her son's killer. He reluctantly agrees but doesn't believe he can really help.

Before long he is plunged into a world of corruption, deceit and greed. His journey takes him from the underbelly of Glaswegian society to the rural idyll of a millionaire's mansion.

Along the way, a death close to home ensures that he has a personal reason to face the dangers and bring the murderer to justice.

Available in paperback and for the iPad and Kindle

The Reluctant Detective returns

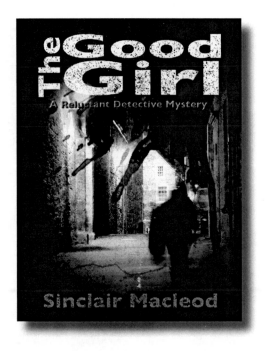

Craig Campbell leaves his native city to investigate the disappearance of a young woman from St Andrews. Initially, it appears to be a simple case of a girl escaping to start a new life but it soon becomes apparent that there are ominous undertones.

When a woman's body is found on a nearby beach the case takes an even darker turn. Craig focuses his attention on the seedy world of escorts and their clients. A pimp with a violent history and a number of witnesses with their own secrets to protect block his investigation.

He finally breaks through the wall of lies and discovers a gruesome truth that leads to a dramatic and explosive climax.

Available in paperback and for the iPad and Kindle

Lightning Source UK Ltd.
Milton Keynes UK
UKOW031046030513

210138UK00007B/139/P